Some of the people who have enjoyed the
STROGANOFF novels
of Caryl Brahms & S.J. Simon:

Alan Coren, Editor of *Punch*

"Sheer joy! Not just the first book for
balletomanes *and* balletophobes, but, quite
simply, a book for anyone who wants to roll
helplessly in the aisles."

Sir Anton Dolin, C.B.E.

"The wittiest, most brilliant books on Ballet
—that Caryl Brahms knew and understood
with uncanny knowledge and real love."

Christopher Fry, C.B.E.

"The delight to be got from the Stroganoff
novels meant that I could never keep them
on my shelves. Friends urgently borrowed
them. Perhaps now they will kindly buy their
own copies and leave me to chuckle in
peace."

Sir John Gielgud, C.B.E.

"It is good to hear that these successful
spoofs are to be republished in America
where I'm sure the sharp wit will be much
appreciated by theatre buffs and balletomanes alike."

Sir Alec Guinness, C.B.E.

"Witty lady — witty books."

Sir Peter Hall, C.B.E.

> "Wit is a rare commodity in this unfunny world. It's here."

Dame Alicia Markova

> "Witty and hilarious books, based on truth."

Jhn Mortimer

> "Witty and elegant fantasies. A great joy."

Moira Shearer

> "My frustration is as great as ever. Why didn't I dance with the Ballets Stroganoff?"

Andrew Lloyd Webber

> "One of the funniest books I have ever read."

Of course, you don't have to be British.

IPL Library of Crime Classics®
proudly presents
STROGANOFF IN THE BALLET
by
Caryl Brahms & S.J. Simon

A BULLET IN THE BALLET

MURDER A LA STROGANOFF
(British title: CASINO FOR SALE)

SIX CURTAINS FOR NATASHA
(British title: SIX CURTAINS FOR STROGANOVA)

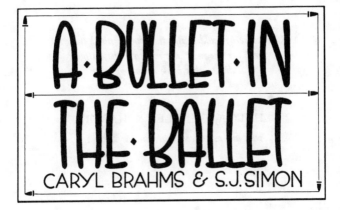

A·BULLET·IN THE·BALLET

CARYL BRAHMS & S.J.SIMON

INTERNATIONAL POLYGONICS, LTD.
NEW YORK CITY

*Overcome by sudden affection due to not having to
meet for the next six months, the authors
dedicate this book to one another*

Also to

HELGA, CHARLES & HAROLD

who are convinced that but for them . . .

Library of Congress Card Catalog
No. 84-80237
ISBN 0-930330-129
Printed and manufactured in the
United States of America.

Second Printing, 1987

PREFACE

by Ned Sherrin

An entry for January 8th 1940 in Caryl Brahm's diary records "...To lunch with Skid (S.J. Simon) at *Canutos*. Oysters. Together we composed the blurb of our Penguin (paperback) edition of *A Bullet In The Ballet*. 'Lunatics of genius'. 'Gifted idiots'. 'Cracked brained collaborators'. 'Impudent wits'. These and similar aspersions have been cast at the heads of Caryl Brahms and S.J. Simon by an admiring press. It is sad to note that this is maintained even when the authors pride themselves that they have been poignant' ...is the way we began it...".

Together Caryl Brahms and S.J. Simon wrote ten novels and a collection of short stories. Their collaboration began modestly in the Thirties when they supplied captions for a series of cartoons by Low in the Evening Standard—Mussolini, the main character, became "Musso—the Home Page Dog", after protests from the Italian Embassy. At the time Caryl Brahms was also, along with Cyril Beaumont and Arnold Haskell, a leading Ballet Critic, while S.J. Simon was the wittiest and one of the most authoratative writers on Bridge. He played for England and his book *Why You Lose At Bridge* is still a classic.

Although they were about the same age, their backgrounds were very different. Caryl Brahms was born in England in 1901—the only daughter of Henry Abrahams, a jeweller, and his wife, Pearl. It was her mother's comfortable Sephardic life-style which coloured her perception of herself.

Her grandmother, Sultana da Silva, was born in Constantinople where her brother was physican to the Sultan of Turkey. Sultana married a merchant, Moses Levi, who divided his time between London and Constantinople. In the course of these annual visits, twenty-one children were conceived—eleven survived. Eventually—probably in 1873—Sultana decided to join her husband. She packed her brood on a coal boat and sailed for England, landing at Liverpool. There she telegraphed a surprised Moses who fetched his family and installed them in a big house in Surrey. After a stormy courtship—the storms came from Sultana —Henry Abrahams and Pearl set up house in a large bungalow on the Island of Canvey, on the Essex coast of the River Thames. Their only daughter, Doris Caroline, precocious, musical and steel-bespectacled, had a haphazard education which included dancing lessons. Most of her knowledge was acquired by surreptitious reading —her mother disapproved of books and thought her daughter's time would be better employed "in embroidery on my tambour, like my cousins". Her parents had marked her out as a suitable companion for her mother; but Caryl inveigled them into sending her to the Royal Academy of Music. Although she could not bear to hear herself play— "I was too musical and already a critic", she was to write later—she enjoyed the social life of the Academy, the escape from home and the opportunity to publish light verse in the Academy's magazine—to some extent this whetting of her literary fingers parallels all those American lyric writers, Ira Gershwin, E.Y. Harburg, Howard

Dietz, etc., who penned brief stanzas for the glory of appearing in F.P. Adams's column in *The Conning Tower.* Having discovered a facility for writing, Caryl Brahms began to publish child verses, initially for women's magazines, shortening her second name from Caroline to Caryl—a usefully unisex spelling in an age where being a woman could count against her. She changed her surname to Brahms so that her parents would not know what she was doing. In later life she would say of "Doris Abrahams"—"This is a woman I have discarded". Her child-verse took her to the London *Evening Standard.* She was living in rooms let by a friend of her mother's when she met S.J. Simon, a fellow lodger, the idiosyncratic son of an apparently equally idiosyncratic Russian family.

Their inspired pairing matched the purposeful but disorganized Brahms with the anarchic Simon, throwing a responsibility for what order ruled in their writing relationship on Brahms and freeing Simon for the wilder flights of fancy to which she encouraged him.

A Bullet In The Ballet was born when Brahms was summoned to the office of her Managing Editor on the *Daily Telegraph.* A fatalist, she assumed that he was about to give her the sack—she was writing Ballet Criticism for the paper. She asked Simon to come with her for moral support. Arriving early they planned the outline of a novel over coffee as a diversionary tactic. It was to be set in the Ballet. Originally the victim was to be Arnold Haskell, the critic for whom she was filling in on the *Telegraph.* Haskell was to be despatched by tossing him high into the flies of the theatre in a blanket, like the Corregidor in Massine's Ballet *Tricorne,* and finding him dead. When that failed to ring true they changed the Ballet to *Petroushka* and invented their actual victim. By the time that Brahms was due to see her Editor, they had fired a deal of enthusiasm for the idea in one another. When Caryl Brahms emerged, unscathed and unsacked (her interviewer had only wanted to ask her advice about a charitable donation to the Arts) they decided to write the book.

For my money there have been three great English comic novelists of high style this century—Evelyn Waugh, Ronald Firbank and the seamless combination of Brahms and Simon. *A Bullet In The Ballet* was their first book. Apart from their novels with a ballet background they explored the backwaters of English history in *Don't, Mr. Disraeli* (Victorian), *No Bed For Bacon* (Elizabethan), *Trottie True* (Edwardian) and *No Nightingales* which spans the centuries. To all these eras they brought their own highly individual view of history. One book was prefaced "Notice to Scholars: This book is fundamentally unsound". From the critic, Clifford Bax, it brough the immediate response that fundamentally their books are sound —it is only on the surface that they are absurd.

Brahms and Simon continued to write together until Simon's death in 1948. He was taken ill after appearing on a television programme about Bridge. An obituarist remembered him as one of "the most absent-minded people I have ever met. Once he had two haircuts in one morning, having completely forgotten the first". In her memoirs, Caryl

Brahms described him, "with his shock of straight black hair surmounting a face of white dough with black currants for eyes to blink at the objects around him, round, full, succulent lips, mostly with a cigarette spilling over with ash tilted between them, and a couple of chins, generous in mold as in nature. Work with Skid (his nickname) meant, in the main, writing wildly inventive, if insufficiently dragooned Brahms-Simon novels and a certain amount of fictional journalism. I took no part in his Bridge Books, he took no part in my Ballet and Drama Criticism... Skid and I laughed our way through a World War and in doing so forged our reputation...".

She also describes their writing method. "The birth of *A Bullet In The Ballet* was not uneventful. Brahms and Simon arranged to meet on a Wednesday to start their Murder Mystery. Simon had, as usual, forgotten and overslept. Summoned by the telephone bell, he turned out and we began in earnest... In *Bullet* the Brahms-Simon mix was all too apparent. Skid took over the detection and the love scenes and I did the ballet bits. Together we wrote the narrative. Thereafter we were to write all our novels together, save for the occasional descriptive passages which I would write. The work progressed bumpily, punctuated by Woodbine cigarettes and frequent cups of tea, amid storms of wild laughter. Inevitably, Skid being Skid, it started late. It was like a long, laughing, wrangling conversation with both of us jumping in on one another. We would speak lines to each other and laugh at our own jokes until one of us stopped and said 'out'. It would have been a very bad day if we had to tell one another what Stroganoff was going to say or do. We just knew...''.

(Nevajno—their ultra modern choreographer—was based on a Russian whom they overheard in the Acol Bridge Club asking plaintively if anyone could "schange small scheque?'').

"...At the beginning, of course, we knew all too little. That *Bullet* was finished at all was due to the kind offices of a fellow writer. Every time we faltered we set up another murder victim. Finally, the coin dropped. What did other writers do when they got stuck?''.

Caryl Brahms asked a colleague, Ernest Elmore, who already had one crime book to his credit under the pseudonym of John Bude. He advised her to give up. Later he relented and conceded that he often found that he could get round a block by "changing the scene or finding a blood-stained handkerchief''. Brahms concealed Bude's discouragement from Simon and passed on only his constructive criticism.

"Ernest thinks we should try changing the background''. Skid tasted the idea. Skid liked the idea. 'Schange small background', he conceded. So we schanged''.

The book was a success—producing an immediate demand for the two more Stroganoff novels. There was a stage version starring Massine and Baronova—and it was played on radio and television in the Forties. Film rights changed hands many times; but the movie has not been made. The Ballets Stroganoff also appear in the Brahms-Simon collection of Short Stories, *To Hell with Hedda;* and in a novel, *Envoy on Excursion.* In

1980, at the age of 79, Caryl Brahms brought out another volume of Short Stories, *Stroganoff in Company.* Four of the tales concerned her favorite Ballet Company—caught up in a translantic drug smuggling racket, embroiled in Monte Carlo, along the Riviera in La Bazouche, and in New York. For *Punch* she wrote another Stroganoff story set at the Edinburgh Festival.

After Simon's death she continued to write novels by herself. When I met her in the early Nineteen Fifties, she began to work more for the stage, radio, movies and television. (With Simon the novels had overshadowed their occasional work in these fields.) Our collaboration began with a modern restatement of *The Beggar's Opera* for deprived children and an adaptation of the Brahms-Simon Shakespearean novel, *No Bed For Bacon.* We wrote three novels, two collections of Short Stories and a book on lyric writers, *Song by Song,* together.

In the 1960's Caryl was a regular contributor to the English version of the late night "satirical" show, *That Was The Week That Was* which I devised and produced. With Ron Grainer we wrote the title song; and she wrote many lyrics with John Dankworth and other composers for it and its successors. In the theatre we wrote five musicals— *Cindy Ella* or *I Gotta Shoe, Sing A Rude Song, Liberty Ranch, Nickleby and Me* and *The Mitford Girls,* and several plays, the most recent was a *tour de force* for Timothy West, *Beecham.* She continued to be concerned and involved in the Theatre until the end of her life. She made a substantial contribution to the revue, *Side By Side By*

Sondheim; devising a pyrotechnic closing medley of Sondheim's songs to round off that show. She became an energetic Governor of The National Theatre of Great Britain, under Lord Rayne's Chairmanship; and she was about to start work on a new theatre project on the morning she died in 1982. To the end of her life her concern for and encouragement of young artists amounted to a passion and in spite of her sometimes formidable manner—small, stout, eyes permanently hidden behind enormous dark spectacles, sharp-tongued on occasion and always imperious on the telephone —she has left behind a legacy of affection to equal the love and respect in which the books she and S.J. Simon wrote together are held.

Her autobiography will be published posthumously in 1984.

London
1983

Ned Sherrin devised, directed, and produced the television series *That Was The Week That Was* and the theatre revue *Side By Side By Sondheim,* in which he also played in London and New York. With Caryl Brahms, he wrote many musicals and plays for radio, television, and the stage. Their most recent London successes were *Beecham,* starring Timothy West, and *The Mitford Girls,* starring Patricia Hodge. His American TV series include *We Interrupt This Week* and *Song By Song,* both for PBS. His autobiography, *A Small Thing Like An Earthquake,* was published in London in 1983.

CHAPTER I

SINCE it is probable that any book flying a bullet in its title is going to produce a corpse sooner or later—here it is.

Dressed somewhat extravagantly in trousers of red and yellow check. Its white jumper is scalloped with scarlet and jade. It wears a yellow bouffon wig, a Russian clown's hat and undertaker's gloves. It is bending over the top of a booth, its arms swinging limply over the sides. There is a neat little bullet hole in the centre of its forehead.

It died magnificently in the presence of two thousand people, most of whom had paid for their seats.

Petroushka! And on this occasion none other than that famous dancer Anton Palook.

Palook had danced energetically and must have been very annoyed when that bullet robbed him of his curtain calls—six under contract. At any rate Vladimir Stroganoff, though still alive, was definitely furious. For the past two years he had jerked his company safely if hysterically through Australia, Harbin, the Gold Coast and Chicago, and here, on the opening night of his London season, they had gone and bumped off his leading dancer. It was not that he felt any particular affection for Palook, in fact privately he was inclined to think that Palook had been asking for it for years—but good Petroushkas were scarce. If it had been Ernest Smithsky now, who mimed his way so conscientiously through *Lac des Cygnes*, or that English girl with the impeccable technique and the impregnable mother, or Stanley Simpson, his indispensable secretary.

But they had picked on Anton. And *Petroushka* was in the bill again on Wednesday week. And it could not be taken out on Wednesday week for that was to be a gala performance in honour of Benois' birthday. And even though the veteran had declared that nothing would induce him to come over to see

Palook (he who had seen Nijinsky, Bolm, Woizikovsky!), this had been suppressed and all society had promised to be present.

Stroganoff scowled furiously at the clustering stage hands.

"Move the body," he commanded. "*Et vite!* Take it away. Forget it. Prepare the next scene."

Fortunately the audience had no idea of what had occurred. The stage manager had rung down the curtain with commendable promptitude and what's more, kept it down. The more determined of the company, unaware of the disaster, cursed him in a variety of languages and pushed their way to the front of the curtain. The gallery clamoured for Petroushka. Stroganoff, with what he afterwards insisted on describing as great presence of mind, tripped over the tassels to announce that Palook had suddenly been taken ill. Gradually the clamour subsided to a sympathetic murmur and the audience trickled out into the foyer.

*   *   *   *   *

The first interval on the opening night of a ballet season is always an animated affair. The dominant note is one of shrill ecstasy, but the impartial observer may also discern an undercurrent of hysteria, jealousy, fashionable display, posturing, thrusting upon and drawing back. There is a curdling of mothers explaining why other mothers' daughters have got the roles, a preening of other mothers accepting congratulations, a hesitancy of fathers, an edging away of critics, all society, all the intelligentsia and any odd dancer who can stake a claim on the company's hospitality. And not a single strong silent man among the lot.

To-night the hubbub was much as usual, but it was moving definitely towards the doors and concentrating on one topic.

*   *   *   *   *

"I'm simply frantic about Anton," said a man with a flaccid mouth. "Simply frantic, my dear. He must be frightfully ill to miss his curtains."

"Dying, I should imagine," observed his companion drily.

A critic standing nearby endorsed the verdict. He had known Anton for eleven years, he said, and the nearest the latter had ever come to missing a curtain call was when the theatre had caught fire in Santiago and he had had to make do with three.

"A poor performance, I thought," observed a second critic, who did not feel that his august paper could in any way be concerned with what had happened after the curtain came down. "The death scene was singularly unconvincing."

"And his passion for the Doll distinctly lukewarm." said a girl who knew everybody.

"It is," announced a man who knew everything.

Outside, the stage-doorkeeper was fast losing his patience. The clamouring mob around him did not seem to understand plain English.

"No," he said for the hundred and fifth time. "You cannot see Mr. Palook."

"But he's expecting me."

"I've got an appointment."

"I always see Anton after a performance."

"I'm Petunia Patch of the *Daily Distraught* and I want to ask him . . ."

"Mr. Stroganoff said that . . ."

"The press agent told me to . . ."

"We want to know how dear Anton is . . ."

"He's dead," said the stage-doorkeeper, his patience evaporating. He regretted it immediately, as half a dozen determined critics, their copy already in the office, pushed their way past him and started fighting for his telephone.

*   *   *   *   *

But the show must go on. This is unfortunate as the next ballet is by that advanced choreographer Nevajno, and depicts Ajax laboriously wrestling with the lightning to Tschaikovsky's "1812." So though poor Anton is in his dressing-room together with a balleto-medico (who for once has found no difficulty in diagnosing the cause of death), Mr. Saintly the manager, Stroganoff and his secretary Stanley Simpson, the audience are back in their seats and the curtain has been rung up on a miscellaneous collection of rocks.

But though the critics must stay and watch, we are under no such obligation.

CHAPTER II

THE Flying Squad tourer pulled up outside the Collodium stage door, tactlessly omitting to make that fascinating noise that accompanies police cars on the screen, and with adequate rapidity disgorged its occupants. These consisted of two police photographers, a police surgeon, Detective-Sergeant Banner and Detective-Inspector Adam Quill.

Detective-Inspector Adam Quill is due to loom largely throughout this narrative, so it might be as well to pause and look at him now.

Detective-Inspector Adam Quill is a serious young man who has joined the police force as a careerist. The first thing you notice about him is his height, which is six foot three, the second his good looks, which are those of the *matinée* idol stamp, lacking only the practised profile that distinguishes the latter. Fair hair, a good-humoured mouth, large capable hands and an unemotional manner. Not supernaturally intelligent but not naturally stupid, he started life as one of Lord Trenchard's young men and has only just managed to live this down, mainly by calling everybody in sight "Sir." He is not altogether without experience, this is his second big case since his Inspectorship (in the first he arrested the wrong man) and this time he is determined to be more careful. He is not a man much given to advance speculation, but judging from the cold precise message received over the 'phone from the theatre manager, Mr. Saintly, it does not seem to him that this case will present many difficulties. From what little he knew of the stage, actors were a jumpy crowd and it should be a matter of mere routine to discover a suspect to fill the three cardinal clauses in the Detective's Handbook—"Means, Motive, Opportunity." As likely as not, he reflected, he would be greeted by some hysterical young woman already in the throes of repentance.

But he was, in fact, greeted by the stage-doorkeeper, who refused to let him in.

Fortunately Stroganoff appeared in time.

After the preliminary greetings, Quill expressed a wish to examine the scene of the crime. The request seemed to puzzle Stroganoff.

"Poor Anton," he said. "He is in his dressing-room for the last time."

Quill looked up sharply. "I thought he was shot on the stage."

"*Mais naturellement*," agreed Stroganoff. "On the roof. It was lucky," he added, "that it was the end of the ballet, so the audience they know nothing and are happy."

"Then you've moved the body?"

"*Mais naturellement*," said Stroganoff, appearing even more puzzled than before. "You cannot have a body in *Ajax* and anyway the *décor*, it is different."

"Am I to understand," asked the persevering Quill, "that you have moved the body and calmly gone on with the performance?"

"*Mais certainement*," said Stroganoff with evident self-satisfaction. "We are well-organised, yes?"

"But were you not aware," asked Quill coldly, "that in a serious matter like a shooting, nothing should be touched until the police have arrived?"

"Sure!" Stroganoff nodded so affably that Quill felt certain he had not understood a word.

"In England the police like to see everything as it was at the time of the event. And now this is no longer possible."

"*Mais oui*," beamed Stroganoff. "*Pour nous tout est possible.* All will be put back on Wednesday week."

This was too much for Quill. "Wednesday week?"

"Sure—we give *Petroushka* again then. For Benois himself. Though who shall dance Petroushka now that Anton is dead I cannot decide. Pavel Bunia, perhaps, but then maybe he is too young—no?"

"No," agreed Quill involuntarily. The patter was catching and it was Stroganoff himself who switched the conversation back to the main subject.

"But you wish to see poor Anton—yes? I will take you. He is in his dressing-room. The star's dressing-room. It was in his contract. I will give it now to Pavel, and if Rubinska's mother, she is angry—poof—that does not matter."

Accompanied by his photographers, the Police Surgeon, and Sergeant Banner—the latter reluctantly detached from his fascinated study of Ajax's defiance—Quill followed Stroganoff up the stairs into the dressing-room. This, at first sight, appeared to combine the functions of the sorting department of a post office with the salient features of the Chelsea Flower Show. There was a smother of photographs of Palook's old dancing masters, his dancing partners, his dancing pupils, the whole culminating in a large and slightly repulsive oil painting of Palook himself in the last act of *Giselle*. The dressing-table was railed off by a curtain, drawn to reveal the usual assortment of dirty towels, cold creams, mascara, rouge and false eyelashes. The golden *Sylphides* wig, due to be worn at to-morrow's performance, was already laid out awaiting the wig-groomer's attention. But readers are asked to suppress the gulps in their throats. They did not see Palook's *Sylphides*—it was horrible.

On the sofa, nonchalantly covered by a Spanish shawl (*Tricorne*), lay the body of the dancer. The fair-haired young man, who had been sitting on the chair beside it, sprang to his feet as the procession entered.

"Stanley," said Stroganoff sharply. "Why are you not in the box watching the performance for me? Go away. You must not interfere with the Inspector who has come to arrange an assassin for us."

Quill quite liked this novel angle on his duties, but as his staff seemed to be enjoying it too, he suppressed his smile and walked over to the sofa.

"Where," he enquired, "is the doctor who examined the body?"

"Gone back to see the ballet," volunteered Stanley Simpson. "Stalls—eleventh row—side. I made a point of enquiring in case you wanted him," he added with evident pride.

"Call him," said Quill.

Stroganoff was delighted to see Stanley go. He was always delighted to see Stanley go. Stanley had no vision—only a head for figures—and figures were easily the most unpleasant factor in Stroganoff's life. Sunnily he turned to the Inspector.

"You have everything—yes? Then I go to rub up my speech."

"Just a moment," said Quill. He turned to the Police-Surgeon who had by this time completed his examination.

"Perfectly straightforward," said the latter. "Shot at a range of about ten yards or over. Death instantaneous. I suppose you'll want the bullet, so let's take the body away and get on with it."

Quill nodded and the body was duly carried out, though not without a howl of protest from Stroganoff, who argued that he needed the corpse's costume for the next presentation.

By this time Quill had an uneasy feeling that the proceedings were not going to be as straightforward as he had supposed. As yet he had but the vaguest idea of the setting of the crime. He knew that it had taken place on the stage, towards the end of a ballet called *Petroushka*, and that the victim was on some sort of roof—why or how he had yet to ascertain. Palook, he understood, was an important person, which meant presumably that he had his fair quota of enemies. He had been shot in full view of the audience, but the range of the shot eliminated the further parts of the house and it seemed unlikely that anyone in the stalls or circles could pull a gun and get away with it. There remained the boxes, the orchestra, the wings and possibly the stage itself, assuming the scenic structure permitted. He would get that scene reset sometime, and before Wednesday week at that!

Manfully he set himself to discover further details. This took rather a long time for at first Stroganoff flatly refused to believe that Quill did not know *Petroushka* intimately, and when finally convinced, showed a strong tendency to take him through the ballet step by step. In this he was energetically assisted by the balleto-medico who had arrived with a heated criticism of *Ajax* on his lips and appeared only too eager to lay his forty years of ballet-going experience at the detective's feet. At the end of twenty minutes Quill began to collect a hazy impression that Palook had thoroughly deserved to be murdered if only because he was no Nijinsky.

Somehow he managed to gather that Palook had died at the moment when Petroushka dies in the ballet. He had been standing on some sort of a roof. The stage, save for some sort of a magician, was deserted, but a few minutes previously it had been overflowing with the entire cast plus a large number of extras. Palook had been standing centre stage in full view of the audience. No shot had been heard, which argued a silencer, and as the position stood, any one of about two hundred people might have done it.

"But," finished Stroganoff, "you will see for yourself what a good work it is. You lucky, lucky man—what an ecstasy there is coming to you. It is arranged then, that you come to my box on Wednesday week. And afterwards," he added as one conferring a great honour, "I introduce you to Rubinska."

"I am afraid," said Quill apologetically, "I shall have to see it before Wednesday week. In fact I would like you to re-enact the scene for me at once. Just as it was at the time of the performance, with everybody who was on the stage then, on the stage now."

"*Pardon?*" said Stroganoff, startled at last.

Quill, in a slow, clear voice, repeated his request. At the fourth time Stroganoff understood.

"*Impossible*," he said in triumph. "First there is Palook. He is dead."

"One of my men will substitute for him."

"But it is a role *bien compliqué*," protested Stroganoff. "No policeman will be able to dance it, even if he could learn quick enough."

At this point the balleto-medico, recovering his sanity, explained to Stroganoff that what Quill wanted was not so much a dancing performance as a reconstruction of the crime. He wanted to see the stage as it was at the time of the shooting.

"But my company is tired," said Stroganoff. "Come to-morrow and all shall be prepared. *Mais moi—je ne vois pas la nécessité.*"

"It is very necessary," said Quill. "And I would prefer to have it now."

"To-morrow at twelve," said Stroganoff firmly. "And even so it is a great favour I do you, for we should at that moment rehearse *Giselle*." He regarded Quill with a new ray of hope. "You would not come to *Giselle* instead—no? It is very beautiful."

But Quill was spared the embarrassment of an answer by the appearance of Stanley, who announced that *Ajax* was over and that the audience, while not exactly clamouring for Stroganoff, were nevertheless making sufficient noise to warrant his appearance before the curtain.

"I come," said Stroganoff. "I have a speech to make," he explained to Quill. "Stanley he wrote it. It is bad. I think I make another. You come and listen."

And, linking his arm affectionately through Quill's, he propelled that resistant figure down the stairs and planted him firmly in the wings. Though why, he asked himself in astonishment, he should take so much trouble over a man who had never seen *Petroushka*. . . . *Tout de même c'était un beau garçon.*

The fascinated Sergeant Banner edged his way through and ranged himself beside his superior. This was life.

*　　*　　*　　*　　*

As he listened to Stroganoff's lyrical improvisations, from which the only fact to emerge clearly was that this night was the greatest night ballet had ever known and would ever know —until Wednesday week, Quill found himself wondering uneasily where his next step in this mad world would lead him.

CHAPTER III

IT was perhaps as well that Palook could not remain alive to read his own obituaries, for he would not have been at all pleased with the manner in which these were framed. By an unfortunate coincidence Hitler had selected the day of his death to threaten the world with peace, collaring the greater part of the front pages and every first leader in the country. This left a mere double column for Palook's sensational end, and much of this had been used up by the sob-sisters with graphic descriptions of everybody's reactions to the event, except, of course, Palook's. There were also obituaries which meanly dragged up the matter of his three unsuccessful marriages, that disastrous season with Balieff, his broken contracts, and the seven times he had walked out on, and crawled back to, Stroganoff. Not an *entrechat*, not a *cabriole*, not so much as one of his six magnificent turns mentioned. Here and there came a grudging admission that his line was good, but this was invariably followed up by a slur on his elevation.

Neither did Palook fare much better on the posters. The morning papers ranged from "Mystery Death of Dancer" to "Well-known Dancer Dead," while in the sporting editions he was entirely obliterated by the gloatings of sundry racing correspondents. (Hector napped Hippopotamus. Won 7-2.)

But even though the world at large did not seem unduly perturbed by its shattering loss, in Palook's own world the reaction was highly satisfactory. Up in the classrooms of the Collodium theatre everybody was in tears. Twenty-six dancers in the *corps de ballet*, fifteen mothers, three fathers, twelve small-part dancers, six *danseuses etoile* and six ballerinas were all refusing to lend each other handkerchiefs. Two ballerinas, who, owing to Stroganoff's beaming vagueness, both claimed to be *assoluta*, were exchanging tears with the pianist, who was herself too upset to utilise the occasion to suggest a small loan. Two bright young journalists—not allowed to be bright this morning—a distraught sugar daddy, absently fondling the wrong pair of shoulders, The Only Man Who Knew About Ballet, and The Only Woman Who Flatly Disagreed With Him, had made their way early to the scene of lamentation. There was Stroganoff edging away from Stanley but bumping into Mr. Saintly, who kept asking his views on the probable box-office reactions. And finally there was Arenskaya, ex-ballerina to the Maryinsky theatre (ex-mistress to Anton Palook), director of classes to the Stroganoff ballet and sole dictator to her husband P. Puthyk. Shrivelled but arrogant she is sitting upright in a gilded chair (*Good Humoured Ladies*) presiding over the mourners. One hand is using Stanley's handkerchief to wipe her eyes, the other eluding the sympathetic pats her husband is endeavouring to administer.

"*Laisse-moi*," she says. "I am inconsolable. I want nothing. Go and fetch my bag that in my distress I left on Stroganoff's table, my cigarettes which are in my dressing-room, and my shawl which I left at home. I am freezing."

P. Puthyk, *Premier Danseur* to the Maryinsky theatre, 1895, *maître de ballet* to every European house in somewhat convulsive rotation, and principal walker-on to the Stroganoff Company, ambled happily off. "Her shawl," he mumbled. "Her cigarettes. And something else which I will remember later."

"*Vite!*" shouted Arenskaya through force of habit.

"*Vite, moia krassavitsa,*" agreed the old man, slowing down to exchange greetings with a new member of the company who still thought he was someone important. He was not nearly so affable to Pavel Bunia who bumped into him in the doorway. That Pavel did not like women was his misfortune; that he had liked Palook no longer mattered; but that he should claim to dance *Le Train Bleu* better than Dolin—that was intolerable. The conceit of it. The impertinence. The young man must be put in his place. He, Puthyk, would do it.

"*Pardon,*" he said coldly, and scuttled off.

Pavel was not noticeably damped. He presented a languid cheek to Stroganoff and the backing Stanley, and sauntered towards Arenskaya.

"Poor Anton," he sighed. "Terrible. I assure you I did not shut my eyes all night. Little did I think when we came to London that it should be I who would dance Petroushka."

Half a dozen heads jerked up sharply at this statement, among them Kasha Ranevsky, a newcomer to the company, who had hoped vaguely that he might secure this distinction. Noticing his depression, Arenskaya beckoned him over, but not, as it transpired, to offer consolation.

"Where," she asked, "is Rubinska this morning? What have you done with her?"

Kasha protested ignorance.

"Nonsense. Bring her at once," commanded Arenskaya.

"She is a bad girl. Last night in *Petroushka* she was four beats late with her entrance. And for why?"

"Er—I'm afraid that was my fault."

"Of course it is your fault. That is what I am saying."

"You whisper in the wings," interposed Stroganoff, "and—poof—she is late. Do not do it no more." He dismissed the young man airily and bent over Arenskaya.

"*Ma belle*," he said, "presently there comes here a young man who has never seen *Petroushka*. But a good boy *quand même*. He is from the police and will catch our assassin. We must help him all we can. It is for him that we do the last act of *Petroushka* this morning."

"Why only the last act?" asked Arenskaya really hurt. "Is the rest not good enough for him?"

"It is not for the dance that he comes to see," explained Stroganoff. "It is because, because . . ." In vain he tried to remember just why it was Quill had insisted on the reconstruction. "Still that is not important. What I wish to say is that this young man will surely ask you many questions."

"The police they always ask questions," nodded Arenskaya from a vast store of mixed experience. "But this time I am not afraid. My passport it is perfect."

"You must be careful what you tell him."

"Me—I am discreet."

"Of course, darling," said Stroganoff, "but you like to talk—no? So do not tell him our secrets—that Rubinska, she is over seventeen, nor that I have not yet signed the contract with America, that I am almost obligated to Cochran to dance at the Trocadero, and that Anton want to leave us to form his own company with that man with the newspapers who takes my ballerinas out to supper and lends me money."

"Excuse me, sir," interposed Stanley, "but I think you have got the wrong idea of the sort of questions the police are likely to ask."

Stroganoff looked at him with deep annoyance.

"You can tell them if you like that Stanley will be leaving us soon."

Stanley laughed heartily in his English way at what he supposed was a joke, and continued:

"They will be more interested in the mechanics of the crime. I shall be able to give them a lot of help there. I have been working out some calculations on muzzle velocity this morning. And then, of course, they will be looking for a motive. That means they will want to probe into Anton's life, his friends, his enemies, his affairs. That is where you will be able to give them information."

"But of course," agreed Arenskaya. "Me—I will tell them how cleverly I seduce Anton ten years ago."

"Poof," said Stroganoff, "they will not be interested."

"*Mais c'était très intéressant*," protested Arenskaya. "Palook, he did not want. He *mauvais sujet*. Havelock Ellis he have chapter about it."

Stanley blushed. He could never quite get accustomed to these franknesses though he came up against them on an average of fifty times a day.

"I would suggest," he began.

"You are always suggesting," said Stroganoff. "Go away."

"It is time we start the class," agreed Arenskaya. She rose and clapped her hands imperiously.

It would be an exaggeration to say that an instantaneous silence settled on the room. In fact nobody took any notice. However, with the aid of much thumping with her stick, some energetic shooing by Stroganoff, and a bleat or so from Stanley, the handkerchiefs were at last abandoned and there was the usual scuffle as to who should lead the *barre*. The young Rubinska, who had only just entered, came off badly in the contest. She looked pale and tired as she made her way listlessly to an inconspicuous position by the mantelpiece.

"Stop," said Arenskaya to her. "You are late. But I excuse you. In fact I forgive you. You will lead the class. And you," she turned to the fat girl, who had planted herself firmly at the head of the *barre*, "go back. Right back," she added and glared defiantly at the fat girl's mother.

There are two types of teachers. The first give the class their *battements* early in the lesson, thus reducing them to pulp and leaving them no energy for the remainder; the second give their class hell all the way through, reserving *battements* as the final torture. Arenskaya belonged to either according to her mood. To-day she gazed long at the ceiling in search of inspiration while the class got peacefully through their *pliés*.

"*Battements*," she said evilly. "First *des petits* and then *des grands*."

The pianist struck a weary chord and the scufflings started. That Palook was dead was no longer important.

* * * * *

Meanwhile Quill at his breakfast table gazed with revulsion at a plate of cold cereals and wondered why he, who faced cut-throats, blackmailers and con. men unflinchingly should lack the courage to give in his notice to Miss Treackle. In front of him was spread the accumulated data of the crime, acquired with superhuman pertinacity. He had obstinately remained in the theatre till 4 a.m., relentlessly turning down Stroganoff's suggestions of a bite of supper somewhere, and ignoring the many flattering glances that fell his way from all and sundry. He had set out on what seemed to him the fairly simple task of collecting the names and addresses of the company who had been around the stage at the time of Palook's death. But many of the company had left the theatre, and though everybody knew with whom everybody else was living, they were all very vague as to where they were doing it. On top of this there had been an undeniable tendency to regard him as an emotional outlet and also a heaven-sent ally in their private fights with Stroganoff. Altogether an exhausting evening.

Still he had made some progress. He had the cast of *Petroushka* and their addresses. The full medical report would be to hand shortly, and he was due to witness the reconstruction of the last act this morning. After that it ought to be a straightforward matter of docketing the data and sifting the evidence.

Grimly he rose to his feet, buckled on his raincoat, and strode out. An eager Sergeant Banner was waiting for him at the stage door.

"They're upstairs," said the sergeant, "little bits of things most of them."

They arrived in the classroom to find the company ranged expectantly in the centre of the room in rows, waiting while Arenskaya had it out with the pianist.

"When I say 'ta-ra-ra,'" she was screaming, "I mean 'ta-ra-ra' and not 'to-ro-ro.' You—you play 'tootle-ootle-oo' all the time. Now then once more."

The girls went miserably back to their series of predicaments, while Quill, and the slightly less fascinated Sergeant Banner, took in the practise costumes, which included many-coloured pullovers—mostly in a state of disrepair—worn over scant tunics and whatever coloured tights happened to be to hand. The hair was worn back from the ears and kept in place by nets and bandeaux. Ubiquitous thighs were encased in knitted pullovers. Feet, that looked so dainty on the stage, appeared long and bony in darned pink satin ballet shoes. Save possibly in the bosom of a mother, ecstasy is not one of the emotions that is evoked by the spectacle of a dancer working in class.

Feeling uncommonly clumsy in the face of so much precarious balance, Quill edged his way over to Stroganoff and tapped him on the shoulder.

"Go away," said Stroganoff absently. He thought it was Stanley.

But Arenskaya, catching sight of the good-looking young

man, stopped the class and came towards him with a slow but very determined gait.

"I am Arenskaya," she announced. "Meet me."

"Ah," beamed Stroganoff into whose consciousness the aura of the detective had at last penetrated. "It is our nice young man who has never seen *Petroushka*. You have slept well—no?"

"I did not close an eye," declared Arenskaya. "First there was poor Anton and then there was my husband who would keep on talking. Here he comes—the villain," she added as Puthyk came hurrying up with a cushion, a small valise and a footstool. "And this you bring—what is it? I did not ask for these things."

"Poof," said Stroganoff. "They will do just as well. And if not, we send Stanley."

He glanced incredulously at his elbow. But for once Stanley was not there. He was at the moment measuring up the stage with a foot rule thoughtfully purchased for that purpose at Woolworth's this morning.

"Never mind Stanley," said Arenskaya. "It is not him that M'sieu have come to see. It is me. He and I we have business together. We go to my dressing-room while my husband take the class."

"*Enchanté*," said Puthyk with alacrity and happily started shouting a number of muddled orders.

"He is a good teacher," smiled Arenskaya as she propelled Quill through the door. "Not as good as me, but still good. He knows my method." She threw open the door of her room. "Now we have a nice little chat while Stroganoff he go down and prepare the stage."

But Stroganoff, into whose plans the idea of a *tête-à-tête* between Quill and the loquacious Arenskaya had definitely not entered, seemed unwilling to relieve the pair of his tactful chaperonage.

"I," he began.

"You," said Arenskaya, drawing herself up and screaming,

"You are impossible. I have worked for Mordkin, Reinhardt, Ziegfeld and all, and you are more lazy than any of them. *Petroushka* yesterday was a disgust. Not only did you allow poor Anton to die, but the bear he come on like a fox terrier. Here is a young man who will see *Petroushka* for the first time, and you—are you interested? No. You care nothing. You are not an artist. Only a man of business."

Though he realised that this was intended as a crushing insult, Stroganoff felt vaguely proud. It was the first time anybody had called him a business man. Off he trotted to boast about it to Stanley.

Alone with Arenskaya, Quill began to feel more normal.

He was about to interrogate a witness, which, as every reader of detection is aware, is the groundwork of any murder case. True this particular witness was not exactly the normal type. Yet, separated from her chaotic companions, it should still be possible to handle her along the lines laid down in the Detective's Handbook.

The first rule was to put the witness at ease, but it was early evident that this would not be necessary. Already Arenskaya was seated in a chair and was waving him to another. (By rights he ought to have been asking her to sit down.) She was offering him an evil-scented cigarette. (By rights he ought to have been asking her if she cared to smoke.)

"Now," she said comfortably, "you tell me all about it."

Quill remembered the second rule: let the witness talk. This witness needed very little encouragement. Already she had expressed an admiration for the appearance of the London Police and was well on the way to expressing her lack of admiration for passport officials, who had been very unreasonable over a matter of an unnotified change of address, caused by an awful landlady, who could not make coffee, who stole her underclothes, and who still expected to be paid. Now she always stayed at an hotel—a good hotel—the Savoy she believed it was called.

Quill jerked hopelessly at the only thread that might turn the conversation into the channel he desired.

"Was Palook living at the Savoy?"

"No," said Arenskaya. "He lived with Pavel. It is disgusting that he still like men after I go to all that trouble to seduce him."

Quill pricked up his ears.

"You were in love with him?"

"Me?" said the astonished Arenskaya. "But no. We sleep a little that is all—me, I love only my husband."

"And did your husband know of this—er—liaison."

"*Pardon*," said Arenskaya. "But of course he know. Everybody know. My husband tell me himself it would be no good, but I do not listen."

But perhaps this husband was not as *complaisant* as Arenskaya made him out. Had he stumbled on a possible motive?

"And when did this happen?"

"Oh—it is now ten years. You must understand I am now old. I do not have many lovers now. But at your age it was different. I must tell you the time when the Grand Duke he . . ."

With difficulty Quill managed to ward off the reminiscence. (Rule 5. Keep the witness to the point.)

"Where," he asked firmly, "were you at the time of the murder?"

"In my box," said Arenskaya. "With Stroganoff—no, Stroganoff he leave before the end."

"Then you saw Palook die?"

"Yes, and for once he die beautifully—right in the middle of the beat."

"Did his death strike you as in any way unusual?"

"But very unusual. As a rule Palook he die two beats too late. But me, I thought it was a fluke. It was only afterwards I realise that somebody shoot him in good time."

"Who told you?"

Arenskaya reflected. "It was Rubinska, I think, yes, I am sure. She was crying when I go to her room to tell her how bad she dance, so *naturellement* I ask what is the matter. I am soft-hearted—*moi*. And she tell me that Palook was shot."

"And how did she know?"

Arenskaya shrugged. "I do not ask. Maybe she shoot him. Oo knows?"

"Would she have any reason to shoot him?"

"We Russians we do not need a reason," declared Arenskaya. "She loved him. That is plenty. And Palook, he no longer love her. That is more than too much."

Quill could almost feel the text book nodding approvingly at him.

"He had left her for another woman?"

"*Pas exactement*. But he left her."

"And you think she shot him to revenge herself?"

"I think nothing," declared Arenskaya. "Maybe she do— maybe she don't. There are others that did not like Palook. Nobody like Palook except Pavel, and even Pavel jealous of his dance. Anyway," she waved an arm, "he is dead, so let us not talk of him any more. It depresses me."

Quill too felt that he had stood all he could digest from this witness for the moment and was relieved when Stanley's eager face popped round the door to announce that the stage was ready.

CAAPTER IV

STROGANOFF was shocked to hear that Quill had never seen *Petroushka;* we feel uneasily that most of our readers will never even have heard of it. If, then, they are to go on with the story (and frankly we see no reason why they shouldn't) they must, for a clearer understanding, hear about it now. Quill has only to sit through the third act, but we must take you through all the scenes as they are danced. Anyway, it is Art.

The stage is set for a Russian Fair in the Admiralty Square, St. Petersburg, 1830. The square is flanked, to the left and right of the stage, with the curtained façades of booths. These have ample balconies, from which merry-makers wave and shout at the crowd below.

The back of the stage is almost entirely taken up by a long, low booth beyond which the snow-covered roofs of the city can be seen. When the ballet begins, bright curtains are drawn across the booth, but later they will be drawn aside to reveal the rooms that house the three puppets. Petroushka, a traditional Russian clown, the Moor, his richly attired rival, and the Doll, for whose affections they compete—these are the tragic triangle than an old showman—the Charlatan, he is coldly called on the programme—has, by means of his enchantments, brought to life. The magician is old and swarthy—an oriental Pygmalion whose puppets have got strangely out of hand, and blames him for their misdemeanours.

When the curtain rises the stage is filled with a shifting gesticulating crowd—the boisterous merry-makers of a Russian fair-ground. The roystering on the stage is swollen and heightened by the roystering in the music. Robust and reeling bursts of sound make the icy air feel the keener to ruby cheeks and vulnerable toes and fingers, by contrast.

Maids and moujiks, women and children, coachmen, nurses, gipsies and merchants fill the booth-fringed square, drifting enquiringly about the stage, now breaking into a spurt of some traditional dance, now stopping to crowd over to some other point of interest. Then breaking up again, and again that enquiring shifting and drifting.

An organ-grinder churns out a tune from a wheezy hurdy-gurdy. It has a romantic treble and an unpunctual bass. Two street-dancers go through their routine with a practised spontaneity, and the crowd gapes. From the balcony the gipsies and their clientele throw down coins. Presently the dancers pack up. The shifting and the drifting starts all over again—until a sudden roll of drums divides the crowd and holds them agog either side of the stage.

From behind the curtains of the puppets' booth emerges Pygmalion. He pipes a wily tune on a reed, swaying to left and right as the phrases rise and fall, and eyeing the crowd between the passages like a suspicious virtuoso who has presented a rival with a complimentary stall and is now bent on making quite sure that he is still sitting in it.

The curtains of the booth are parted, and lo! three puppets loll inanimate in their separate cells. The Charlatan pipes a perky phrase—a puppet springs magically to life. Another phrase—up pops a puppet. A last perky pip-pip, and all three puppets are eyeing the musical director anxiously. The baton swoops—the puppets, the entire orchestra, and half a hundred balletomanes, who have been waiting for this moment for some seven months or more, plunge into a dance.

Sound crescendos into a stressed stridency. Rhythm quickens. The puppets burst from the cells and take the centre of the stage. Petroushka, white-faced—agonised—nimble as quick-silver. The Moor, horridly affable. The Doll, wide-eyed, scarlet-cheeked, with the fine airs of a gay lady imported to this snowy scene from the warm walls of Paris. The puppets have a child-like directness, and their jerked movements are more convincing than many a naturalistic presentation.

They dance with jerky velocity, compelled by some wild force outside themselves. A vitality born of the crashing spells of the magician. They dance until the fierce cogs of the orchestra seize up.

Comes the black-out.

Comes, as well, a curtain—extremely worn—depicting the Magician taking his ease on a number of comfortable-looking clouds, the emblems of his trade—(you want the finest spells—

we paint them). The initiate hail this faded masterpiece with an ecstatic: "Ah, *le rideau!*" The novice will no doubt fumble with an obstinate match and the obsolete programme notes.

Meanwhile, a roll of drums conducts the audience to the second scene of the ballet—a close-up of Petroushka's cell. Here he is, imprisoned in his black hell. The three dark walls are broken sharply by a white door, a shark's-tooth frieze of icy mountain crags. A picture of the Magician is painted implacably upon the wall—a constant reminder of servitude.

Petroushka is more nearly human than the other puppets, more keenly aware of the division between himself and the meanest of mankind. His arms move—but only by favour of the Magician. His heart pays homage—but in a stuffed frame. His words of love are the miserable slaverings of an idiot. His smile is a pathetic scarlet gash, slipping sideways into self-pity. In his inability to express himself, he is the most articulate figure that the Ballet knows.

While he is screaming his blame at his immediate God—the old Charlatan—the Doll enters. She advances to him on the point, calmly poised, and conscientiously devastating. But the wildness of his welcome terrifies her and "Poof—she run away," as Stroganoff told the fascinated Sergeant Banner. After her startled exit, Petroushka, in an ultimate frenzy, tears down the walls of his cell.

Again the roll of the drums, that is inserted to catch the imagination of the audience and waft it, charged with expectation, to the Moor's cell.

A luxurious apartment, this, walled richly in orange and jade and pomegranate. There is an exotic air of palm and pineapple about the place, and when the curtain rises the Moor is reclining upon a velvet divan, tossing a coconut into the air with his toes, and failing to catch it in his hands.

"But accidents, not always they can happen—though Pavel is toffee-fingers," explained Stroganoff to these receptive lobes, the sergeant's ears. And on this occasion we will take it that the Moor has successfully tossed and caught his toy.

The Moor is richly clothed. Moreover he appears to be steeped in a rather tallowy sex appeal. His name, you could swear, is Pedro.

He catches the coconut, shakes it, rolls his great eyes at it, crouches in homage before it.

Enter the Doll, a tasselled trumpet to her lips. She dances gaily round the stage while a trumpet in the orchestra emits a series of hoots and bubbles on her behalf.[1] This utterly captivates the Moor—or perhaps it is her mixture of sophistication and naïveté. Together they go clumsily through the movements of a *pas-de-deux*. Together they retire to the divan. Together they . . . but what is that shrill sworl of sound?

It is Petroushka.

The Doll faints. The Moor takes to his heels, Petroushka after him. There is a wild fight. The Moor emerges from it first, and flings Petroushka out.

And now we come to the fourth tableau—"The Tableau of Death," as Stroganoff said eerily to the goosey Sergeant Banner.

The Fair is at its height. Egged on by the heightened rhythms in the orchestra, the pink footlights, and possibly the assistant stage-manager, who has been at pains to tear up a large number of paper strips, a rich merchant descends from the balcony to scatter largesse among the merry-makers. He is accompanied by a pair of gipsies who inevitably have a sister act that they feel the urge to put across. A band of nursemaids enter. They dance in the square—one of those traditional dances that flutter with gay inadequate handkerchiefs. A bear lumbers soberly across the stage, chained to a begging-cup. Some coachmen get together. They squat on their heels and throw out their legs, and the audience shouts *"Bis! bis!"* A party of masqueraders, the giant-headed carnival revellers, whip the

[1] "My orchestra—it is perfect": Stroganoff.

gambols to a frenzy. Snowflakes fall softly upon the whirling crowd.

Suddenly the curtains of the puppets' booth are shaken. The shrilling of the puppets is heard. They burst from their booth in a wild death rout. The Moor strikes Petroushka with his scimitar, and, surrounded by the crowd, he dies most piteously in the snow. The crowd gather about the limp body to stare at Petroushka, "And also," Stroganoff explained, "so that Anton, he could crawl away, and the audience, they should not see him."

A watchman is sent for the Charlatan, and soon Pygmalion arrives, summoned from some nice warm tavern where he has been going over those dear old days when he used to show tame bears, instead of temperamental puppets, while the barmaid yawns and pushes across the vodka bottle.

Out in the square it is icy. He is an old man. His public are looking reproachful. They threaten him. It looks like the beginning of a Russian roughhouse. But the old man calms the crowd.

"See," he tells them, "Petroushka is only a puppet. He has no existence outside my art. See . . ." and pushing his way to the back of the crowd, he holds up a limp sawdust puppet.

The crowd laughs. In twos and threes they drift into the gathering shadows. The Charlatan is left alone on the darkening stage, trailing his sawdust puppet.

Then the wild voice of Petroushka screams out above the booth. High on the roof his spirit is seen mocking the magician, until with a last tormented writhe, it, too, collapses as limp as the puppet below in the Charlatan's horrified grasp.

*　　*　　*　　*　　*

But a ballet without an audience is like a cherry orchard after Tchekov has finished with it. The fruit hangs wearily and nobody seems to care how it tastes. The dancers are saving themselves for the evening performance. They go through

their movements conscientiously, but on the flat. The scenery
has a dead look because the lighting has not been adjusted.
The conductor is unleashing all those nasty comments he
would have liked to have made the evening before. The
oboist is looking hurt, the harpist has a cold and the leader
of the third violins hasn't turned up at all. Out in the house,
the stalls under their dust covers stretch wearily across the
auditorium like the dead waves of a white sea. It is almost a
shock in the middle of this vast emptiness to see Stroganoff's
amiable dome, bald and shining, and bobbing about as if it
were in its own office. Beside him Arenskaya is nothing but a
loud voice from a twisted shadow. Quill and the fascinated
Sergeant Banner, the latter firmly planted in the front row,
complete the effect. The curtain has just gone up on the noise
and bustle of the last act.

"*Voilà*," said Stroganoff proudly. "Just as Benois designed it
in 1910 in Paris. Even some of the costumes they are the same."

Quill nodded vaguely. He had the strained expression of a
man who is trying to absorb everything at once. This was
awful. Not a square inch of the stage but had its gyrating
occupant, and none of them seemed to gyrate in one place for
long. From the balconies gipsies waved and mouthed, handsome Russian women cavorted gaily, the crowd pushed and
jostled. Now three energetic coachmen produced an inspired
rough and tumble, but only to give way to Carnival figures
with great heads and beaks, who leapt about the stage getting
in everybody's way. Snow began to fall and the curtains of the
puppet booth, running almost the length of the stage, were
agitated as though by a hurricane. From them burst the
affrighted Doll, the Moor, scimitar raised on high, and a
wizened Petroushka ambling furiously round the stage like a
bumble bee in a hurry.

"*Mon Dieu!*" Arenskaya's shrill voice almost drowned the
miscellaneous noises in the orchestra. "It is my 'usband!
Why?"

Stroganoff, holding her forcibly in her seat with one hand, explained with the other that this was at Puthyk's own request.

"The good old one is always asking me to allow him to dance Petroushka and to-day it cost nothing to give him that pleasure."

Meanwhile, the Moor, unable to postpone catching this rather laggard Petroushka any longer, had killed him several bars too early and had now advanced to the footlights to reason with the conductor.

"You," he said, "you never look at the stage, and if you did it would make no difference."

"You," retorted the conductor, "cannot count nine in a bar when you hear them."

The Moor burst into what sounded to Quill like Arabic. Actually it was Russian. The conductor, an unsubtle soul, called the Moor a bastard. Stanley's anxious head appeared round the wings. It was the last straw. Like a billiard ball Stroganoff shot from his seat, gathered momentum down the gangway, and grasped the conductor ungently by his hair.

"You shall not annoy many more of my dancers," he bellowed. "Through you I was estranged from poor Anton, and now you wish to lose me my Pavel. You watch your stage and you take your time from them. You hear me. And afterwards you are sacked."

"You cannot sack him," hissed Stanley in an agitated undertone. "His contract is watertight."

"Poof," said Stroganoff. "My advocate he soon alter that." He waved his arms furiously at everybody. "Now go on. Proceed. *Continuez*. I have a man here who has never seen *Petroushka* and this is the effect you show him."

Meanwhile, the dead Petroushka had risen, unseen behind the crowd that clustered in front of him, and was being helped up a ladder back stage that led to the top of the booth, where his spirit was due to appear.

B

"*Ostorojno!* Be careful, my darling," shouted Arenskaya who could not see him but knew well what must be happening.

"It is all right," the old man shouted back cheerfully, "I am almost up."

The ballet went on. To a quieter rhythm the stage was cleared of its multitudes till there was only the magician dragging the lifeless effigy of the stock Petroushka across the sawdust. The squeal of the oboe shot through the air, mouthing Petroushka's death agony for him. Immediately Puthyk bobbed up on the roof, waved his arms furiously at Quill, twisted his head frantically in all directions, and finally collapsed in mock death.

"Excuse me," Quill asked Stroganoff, "but did Palook move his head like that in the part?"

"Not like that," said Stroganoff, shocked. "Much better."

This was disappointing, as a twisting head meant that it would be difficult to fix the direction from which the shot had been fired with any certainty. Nevertheless, the reconstruction had served its purpose. There were not many places around the stage where the murderer could have concealed himself to fire unseen at his target. The balconies on each side of the stage were the most probable of them. They had been crowded with performers during most of the ballet and if one of them had elected to stay behind? He had better examine the balconies at closer quarters.

*   *   *   *   *

He arrived on the stage just in time to prevent the stage hands from dismantling it, and began climbing up the stairs that led to the balcony.

"What for you climb up there?" asked the interested Stroganoff. "The ballet it is finished." As Quill did not answer, he followed him, babbling excitedly, up the steps to the balcony where he stumbled over a figure crouched in the shadows.

"Stanley," he said in disgust. "Go away. It is impossible," he complained to Quill, "either he follow me or else he get there first."

But Stanley was far too excited to be squashed.

"Look," he gloated and stretched out his palm dramatically.

"Poof," said Stroganoff unimpressed. "It is a button. I can find you tousands like it."

Stanley withered him with a look and passed his capture—a small pearl button that might be worn by any member of the cast—up to Quill.

"Don't you think," he pressed, "that this was dropped by the murderer?"

Quill smiled at him. He liked this youngster's enthusiasm, which joyously ignored the fact that the scene had been struck and set before the reconstruction.

"It might," he said gently, "but it might also belong to any of the dozen people that have occupied the balcony this morning."

"Shall I check up on the dresses?"

"Don't bother," said Quill. He had an idea. "Tell you what—if you really want to be helpful you might make me a list of all the people who mount this structure during the last scene."

Stanley was clearly delighted. He darted off.

"That," said Stroganoff awed, "was an idea. I will remember him."

The inspection of the balcony was soon completed. As Quill expected, the ledge offered an excellent hiding-place for a murderer. Crouched behind it a person was completely concealed from the wings and stage. He tested this for himself. (Detective's Handbook, Rule 27.)

"Can you see me?" he shouted to Banner.

"No," Banner shouted back.

"Try me from another angle."

Banner took a walk and reported that from one or two places the dim outline of Quill could just be made out.

"You are *drôle*," said Stroganoff amused. "In the perform-ance the lighting it is different or the snow it would not show. If you stay like this down on the floor no one can see you. Anyway no one would want to look while Petroushka die."

Quill felt inclined to agree. If the murderer had indeed selected this spot, the chances were that he had remained un-observed. Probably the conditions on the balcony opposite were much the same. Still, he had better look at them.

The balconies proved to be identical.

"You have finished?" asked Stroganoff hopefully as they descended. "Then we set the stage for *Copélia*. You have seen *Copélia*—no?"

But it appeared that this unnatural person was still not satisfied. He was climbing up on to the roof where Petroushka had stood. Here Stroganoff firmly refused to accompany him. He was too old to climb up ladders, he said, and soil expensive new suits from Savile Row, which Stanley insisted on ordering, and which fitted in all the wrong places.

Quill completed his inspection alone. But beyond a few blood-stains there was nothing to learn.

"Loonch?" asked Stroganoff hungrily as he descended.

Quill excused himself. He wanted a rest from Stroganoff. He was planning a quiet hour of recuperation at a neighbouring pub.

CHAPTER V

BUT Quill was not allowed to recuperate. No sooner had he got outside the theatre than he was joined by a bowler-hatted Stanley, glancing furtively around him.

"Gave old Stroganoff the slip," he announced joyously. "You see I have one or two theories on this case you might like to hear."

Quill accepted the offer and invited him to lunch—on Scotland Yard. Not that he had much confidence in the theories, but there were several questions about the company he wanted to ask, and after all Stanley was English. He steered him to the pub.

"Now," said Stanley comfortably as the waitress departed with the order, "I realise, of course, that everybody connected with the crime is under suspicion. As I'm anxious to help you, it is necessary that I should be eliminated at once from the list. I will therefore give you my alibi."

The astute reader at this point will immediately jump to the conclusion that Stanley must be the criminal and that this ingeniousness is merely low cunning designed to mislead. Even Quill had read enough detective stories to feel vaguely suspicious. However, he merely nodded to Stanley to proceed.

"At the opening of the fourth act," said Stanley, "I was in Stroganoff's box. Presently I said something and he told me to go away. He is always telling me to go away," he added a little sadly. "So I went back stage to have a word with Shura."

"Shura who?"

"Shurra you've been troubled!" said Stanley, succumbing to the temptation. He repented his lapse instantly and became serious. "Her full name is Shura Lubova. She is one of the most promising of our younger dancers and I'm frightfully sorry for her. You see the poor chick has fallen for that bounder Pavel. It's almost a tragedy. So as I knew she was not due on till *Ajax*, I thought it would be a good moment to go to her dressing-room and offer her some advice."

"How did she take it?" asked Quill, waiving his professional duties for the fascinating picture thus conjured up. If this Shura was a younger edition of Arenskaya. . . .

But it appeared that Shura had not been in her dressing-room. Shura, in fact, had generously offered to deputise for one of the gipsy walkers-on in *Petroushka*, and Stanley had arrived in the wings in time to see her mounting the balcony.

He did not speak to her but had stationed himself where he could congratulate Rubinska on her performance when she came off the stage.

Quill consulted his programme. "That's the girl who dances the doll?"

"So you've noticed her," said Stanley delighted. "Of course you can't help noticing her. She's a wonderful person." He coughed modestly. "She's—er—my girl, you know?"

This did not tally with Arenskaya's version.

"I thought she was in love with Anton Palook?"

Stanley said that wasn't serious. Just a passing infatuation she would have got over in any case even if Anton hadn't been murdered. She was just a normal healthy English girl and, after the fascination of being admired by pseudo-celebrities, or Lesbians like Tania Ospova, had worn off, would no doubt fall into his arms. He was positive about it.

Quill hurried to agree.

"So your alibi," he suggested, "is that you were talking to Rubinska when the shot was fired?"

"Not altogether," said Stanley. "As a matter of fact she went straight past without seeing me and young Kasha Ranevsky collared her, he's hopelessly in love with her, poor devil, and they went off whispering. I didn't like to butt in, so I stayed where I was and watched Anton. Curiously enough I was just thinking what a wonderful target he made up there on the roof, when somebody shot him. Rather a coincidence—wasn't it?"

"What made you think of targets?"

"Well," Stanley hesitated, "there's no point in trying to conceal it, Inspector, as you're bound to find out sooner or later anyway—but I'm rather a dab with a revolver. As a matter of fact I practise at the Leicester shooting galleries every week."

"Oh, you do," said Quill amused. "Of course that puts you very high in the list of suspects at once." He smiled. "Now if you'd only tell me that there was nobody standing near you at the time. . . ."

"But there was," said Stanley. "The wings were full of people waiting to take their curtains. I was standing next to the stage carpenter, he's bound to remember it, and beside me were . . ." He enumerated a list of Russian names too quickly for Quill to follow. "Good Lord, if you really suspect me I can bring you . . ."

Quill hastened to reassure him. He pointed out that he had to make certain of everybody's movements and offered Stanley another drink. But by the time he had finished it, Stanley was himself again, and telling Quill proudly that while he had not actually heard the plop of the revolver, he had been one of the first persons to realise that something was wrong, and dash round to the roof. He had also, he said, told Stroganoff not to disturb anything till the police arrived, but the latter had, as usual, told him to go away. So he had accompanied the body to the dressing-room and kept guard over it till Quill had arrived.

Having thus, as he felt, firmly established his innocence he went on to offer his theories of the crime. Quill let him talk, feeling that this was as quick a way of gathering information as any other.

Stanley began by saying that the solution of every murder case lay in the concentration upon the three cardinal clauses: Means, Motive, Opportunity. Quill allowed this infringement of the Detective's Handbook to pass without protest. The means they knew—a revolver with a silencer. Routine work would establish the opportunity, and as for motive, said Stanley, he could think off-hand of a dozen persons with sufficient inducement. Despite *de mortuis nil nisi* and all that it was no use blinking the fact that the late Anton Palook had been a bit of a bounder, in fact a thoroughly nasty bit of work. He had no scruples, no sense of honour, and had never been to a public school. He was both a sex maniac and—er—a homosexual. He quarrelled with everybody and double crossed everyone.

Quill begged him to be more specific.

"Well," said Stanley. "Take Palook and Stroganoff. Stroganoff made Palook. When Stroganoff found him, Palook was a nobody. But was Palook ever grateful? No! He was always making trouble, always demanding more salary, always threatening to leave at critical moments. He did in fact leave him several times, but he always came back. Never did any good alone. But he never learnt his lesson. In fact, this is confidential of course—he had been planning to leave Stroganoff again—this time in a big way—to form his own company and take most of Stroganoff's best dancers with him. As a matter of fact old Stroganoff was quite worried about it. You see, there was a rumour that Palook had persuaded Lord Buttonhooke to back him, and with his money he would, of course, have been able to offer far higher salaries than Stroganoff could afford. So in a way Palook's death is quite a good thing for Stroganoff. Not, of course, that I think for a moment that the old boy did it."

Quill was inclined to agree, but decided to keep an open mind on the matter. It was not that he could not visualise that effervescent Russian letting off a gun at Palook, but he could not see him hitting him.

"Then," said Stanley, "there's Volti-Subito—the conductor. You saw an exhibition of his temper this morning. He and Palook were deadly enemies. They had a row after every performance and rehearsal. Of course you could put it down to artistic temperament, but it always seemed to me that there is something more behind it than that. You might probe into it. And I happen to know that Volti is a first-class shot."

Quill nodded. "Any other suspects?"

There were plenty. It was unpleasant talking about it, but there was no doubt that there was a lot of what Stanley blushingly called "unnatural sex" in the company, and that the passions it aroused seemed far stronger than that produced by its natural counterpart among ordinary healthy Englishmen.

Palook had lately started an intimacy with Pavel—the man who had kicked up that row with the conductor this morning —and the intimacy had reduced Pavel's dresser—a fellow called Serge Appelsinne—to the depths of despondency. Appelsinne was a homosexual who had been superseded by Palook in Pavel's intimacy. Since then he had been going about, muttering gloomily, speaking to nobody, and hardly being able to bring himself to look at Palook. He had even stopped watching him dance. And then there was Pavel himself, who, although a man, seemed more jealous than any woman. Palook recently had been showing some friendliness towards young Kasha Ranevsky and every time Pavel saw them together he threw a fit of hysteria and threatened to kill Palook if he were ever untrue to him. In fact they had had a furious row about it just before the fatal act. Of course, Stanley had not thought anything of it at the time and had not watched Pavel when he came off the stage after dancing the Moor. Had he known that he would find himself assisting Scotland Yard in a murder case he would, of course, have kept his eyes skinned.

Quill did not contradict this self-appointed partnership. The information he was getting was far too valuable. There remained the feminine element. Here in view of his confession, Stanley was likely to be more reticent, so Quill resolved to try to startle him into candour.

"Then," he said, "there is your girl friend—Rubinska. Palook had thrown her over."

The effect was instantaneous. Stanley sat up stiffly and glared at him.

"Absurd," he said coldly. "And anyway it's not what she told me. She said she had decided to cut him out."

"Arenskaya thinks she might be capable of it."

"Arenskaya is an ass," said Stanley firmly. "You might as well suspect Arenskaya herself or that doddering old idiot her husband."

"I do," said Quill. He was satisfied that Stanley's indignation was genuine and that whatever share Rubinska may or may not have had in the murder, there had been no collusion between the two. . . . "I suspect everybody," he explained, "and I suspect nobody for the moment. All I want is facts. Rubinska has a motive of sorts—she may have had opportunity. She was not with you at the time of the shot. I shall examine her in the course of ordinary routine, just as I must see everybody. You understand that surely."

The appeal was successful. Stanley apologised rather sheepishly for his outburst. Quill must understand that he loved the girl. Quill reassured him that he understood.

Stanley now produced a list of the players who had mounted the balcony during the fatal scene, which he assured Quill was complete, and Quill's congratulations on his efficiency in acquiring it more than sufficed to restore him to his usual mood of bright efficiency.

After Stanley had departed, Quill sat over his coffee trying to sort the miscellany of information that had been thrust upon him into some sort of order. All Stanley's statements would have to be checked, of course, but assuming his facts to be correct the situation, as recorded in his note-book, now stood as follows :

Palook had been killed by a revolver shot fired at a range of not less than ten yards, and not more than fifty yards, at the climax of the ballet when all eyes would be on the performers. The shot might have been fired from wings, orchestra pit, circles or stage boxes, but the most likely place was one of the two balconies on the left and right of stage. These were occupied by several members of the cast almost till the moment of the murder. It was possible for the murderer to linger on there after the others had left and make his descent after the final curtain when all eyes were elsewhere. Enquire whether anybody saw person or persons descending from balcony after shot was fired.

List to hand, provided by Stanley, probably not complete, of all persons entitled by the script of the ballet to mount balcony in scene. Check up list and if possible obtain evidence of time of descent of occupants.

If Palook was shot from wings, murderer would need secluded spot. Is there such a place before a final curtain? Investigate. Find out who, in the company, own revolvers.

Motive for murder. According to Stanley there is an abundance of motives. Palook appears to have been the best hated man in the company. Investigate the following:

Stroganoff. Palook was about to form rival company under auspices of Lord Buttonhooke, taking Stroganoff's best dancers. This presumably would mean ruin, therefore ample motive. Check S's movements at time. If in box, find out if in stage box.

Rubinska. Jilted by Palook. Danced doll in *Petroushka*. Found by Arenskaya shortly after murder in dressing-room, very distressed and with full knowledge of events. How did she know? Seen previously by Stanley walking away with Kasha Ranevsky, after first stage death of Petroushka.

Kasha Ranevsky. In love with Rubinska and growing intimacy with Palook (possibly assumed). Danced coachman in *Petroushka*. Seen by Stanley with Rubinska as above.

Pavel. Pervert. Danced Moor in *Petroushka*. Apparently second best hated man in company. Intimate with Palook, but objects to growing friendship between Palook and Kasha. Leaves stage after first death of Petroushka before the end of ballet. Subsequent movements unknown. Find out.

Serge Appelsinne. Dresser and intimate of Pavel. Thrown over by Pavel in favour of Palook. Furiously jealous. Movements at time of crime unknown. Enquire.

Arenskaya. Former mistress of Palook. Claims her husband did not mind. Probably correct but——

P. Puthyk. Husband of Arenskaya. Once famous dancer. Walker-on in *Petroushka* and on Stanley's list as one of the people on left-hand balcony in scene. Question on subject of wife's infidelity and try to gather real feelings.

Shura Lubova. In love with Pavel. Palook would be obstacle to bliss. Has no part in *Petroushka*, but deputised for one of walkers-on. Surely this is unusual. Observed by Stanley mounting left balcony.

Volti-Subito. Conductor. Bad terms with Palook. Motive hardly adequate, but Stanley hints may be other and better grievances. First-class shot. Opportunity to shoot unobserved unlikely, but just possible as all eyes are on stage.

On the whole Quill was fairly satisfied with the morning's work. From a vast babble of sound, the ballet world was beginning to sort itself into a number of well-tabbed cogs, and his next few steps were at any rate reasonably clear. He had to interview the people on his list and confirm and expand the information in his possession.

He called for his bill, paid it, noted the amount on his expenses sheet, and, feeling considerably fortified, walked back to the Yard.

There he learnt that the inquest on Palook was fixed for Friday. Armed with a sheaf of subpœnas he made his way back to the theatre. When this case was over, he promised himself, he would definitely give his notice to Miss Treackle.

CHAPTER VI

BACK at the theatre Quill asked for Pavel and was directed to his dressing-room. The call boy, who had escorted him, retreated a few steps and took up an expectant attitude at the end of the corridor. Quill knocked. There was no answer. Quill knocked again. Nothing happened. Quill thumped. This time the door did open, but only a few inches, and an old ballet shoe whizzed past his ear. It was neatly fielded by the call boy.

Quill began to feel dimly that his presence was not wanted. Nevertheless he knocked for the fourth time.

"In the name of the law," he tried.

It worked. The door was flung open.

"Ah, Mr. Inspector, it is nice of you to call. Why did you not say sooner it was you?" Pavel, revolting in a resplendent dressing gown, gushed a welcome. Behind him a tall bullet-headed man with slanting eyes and high cheek bones, stood in a non-committal silence. This, thought Quill, must be Serge Appelsinne, the jealous dresser.

"Make yourself comfortable," fawned Pavel. "Wiskyan-soda?"

"There is no soda," said Serge grimly, "or whisky."

"Never mind," said Pavel. "We will make you Russian tea instead. Serge—the kettle."

Quill glanced round. The room, though slightly smaller than the dressing room he had seen the previous evening, had much the same atmosphere. There were the same curtains drawn to reveal the same kind of dressing-table, loaded with the same kinds of grease paints. There were the same photographs on the wall, the same wreaths, but smaller, and the same telegrams. There was as yet no repulsive oil painting of Pavel in *Giselle*, but this, one felt, was merely a matter of time.

They drank tea while Pavel sighed over Palook's death.

"He was my best friend," he sighed. "But do not let him hear." He pointed to Appelsinne who had retreated to the wardrobe. "He is jealous—that one."

"Quite," said Quill.

"What an artist!" said Pavel. "What a dancer! His death it is a loss irreparable to the company. It is true that I shall dance Petroushka as well as he—maybe a little better—but who now shall dance the Moor?"

What would Stroganoff say to this, Quill found himself thinking? There was only one answer.

"Poof," he said experimentally.

The effect was electrical. In an instant all Pavel's amiability had departed. He leapt to his feet, livid and quivering, while Appelsinne leapt and quivered beside him.

"The Moor," said Pavel, "it is the most difficult role in the ballet."

"Every educated person knows that," said Serge.

"He is symbolic."

"He has a scene all to himself."

"And a *pas-de-deux*."

"He is subtle. He must depict passion. There is no one in the company except Pavel subtle enough to take him."

"No one," said Pavel with evident satisfaction. He bowed to Appelsinne and sat down.

Quill remembered something.

"What about Kasha Ranevsky?"

Once again Pavel leapt to his feet. Kasha, it appeared, was impossible, a clumsy elephant, no dancer, an artistic calamity, and altogether quite beyond the admittedly broad-minded pale of the Stroganoff company.

"Further," said Pavel, "it is a mistake to suppose that Palook admired him. He was only being kind, and anyway he was no judge of a dancer."

"And yet," said Quill, dropping another stone into the pool of rather savage sorrow that seemed to surround Palook's death, "I was informed that Palook was engaging him to dance leading roles in the new company under Lord Buttonhooke."

Appelsinne laughed derisively. "The new company! That is funny. Very funny. The leading roles. I do not think."

"Now that Anton is dead," explained Pavel, "it is assuredly I who will form the Ballet Buttonhooke, and Kasha will not be in the company at all."

"You think that Lord Buttonhooke will approach you?"

"*Assurément*—he approach me first and while we dispute the contract, Anton he come and offer the double cross."

"*Schwolotz,*"[1] said Appelsinne.

"'That is not kind," said Pavel, reprovingly. "He was not a *schwolotz* only a *merzavitz.*[2] Anyway he is dead and can grab no more contracts. How he grab all the good contracts that man! A genius. Only Stroganoff too much for him."

That seemed to be that. Quill offered his cigarettes, but his gaspers were scornfully waved to one side.

"I would like," said Quill, "to ask you a few questions about the time Palook died."

The two men glanced at each other.

"Alas," they said in unison, "we know nothing."

Quill assured them it was a matter of mere routine. In the case of murder he had to question everybody.

"When you left the stage yesterday," he asked Pavel, "where did you go?"

Pavel pondered. "I stand in the wings to take my curtain."

"Curtains," corrected Appelsinne.

"The left or the right wing?"

"The right."

"And did you take your curtains?"

Pavel pondered again and to Quill he seemed a little uneasy. "*Certainement,*" he said at last.

"Then presumably you did not hear that Palook had been shot till later?"

"Much later," agreed Pavel.

"As a matter of form," said Quill, "did anybody see you standing in the wings?"

"*Mais oui,*" said Appelsinne. "I was with him. I wait for him with the dressing-gown."

"This dressing-gown," said Pavel, proudly.

"Who else was near you?"

Neither of them could remember. There were many people

---

[1] Schwolotz—Swine.   [2] Merzavitz—Scoundrel.

in the wings at the end of *Petroushka*, but they were of no interest. Quill persisted. Surely they must have noticed somebody specific. But neither Pavel nor Appelsinne could remember. They were, they said, far too interested in each other to notice. It was an unsatisfactory statement and, as he rose to go, Quill resolved to have this alibi confirmed by independent witnesses before he accepted it.

The pair ushered him out with solicitude, but to Quill there seemed a certain amount of relief in their bearing at his departure.

*   *   *   *   *

Quill's next call was on Stroganoff. He found the latter in his office talking explosively at a pair of tortoiseshell spectacles and a large cigar.

"Ah," he broke off to beam at Quill. "The man who has never seen *Petroushka*. Meet my press agent—M'sieur Saussisson."

"Sausage," corrected the cigar wearily. "Hiram B. Sausage."

"Saussisson," said Stroganoff proudly, "he hot dog. Very hot dog. But he have no heart. Does he weep for Anton? No. 'Poof,' he says, 'it is good publicity.' He must use. And he say that we give another performance of *Petroushka* damn quick while the iron it is warm. Me I hesitate till Stanley say it is no good—the British public would not like—then I realise that Saussisson is right. So we give extra performance of *Petroushka* on Thursday, and Saussisson he make the publicity."

"Leave it to me," said Sausage. "Handled right the story will stay on the front page of every tabloid for a week." And off he went, presumably to handle it.

"Wiskyansoda?" asked Stroganoff.

But there was no whisky—only Russian tea. This Quill refused firmly. Stroganoff was sorry and poured himself out an enormous glass.

"And our assassin," he asked cosily. "You have found him—no?"

"We are doing our best," said Quill. "The inquest is on Friday." He handed Stroganoff the subpœna. Stroganoff examined this with interest.

"What is that?"

Quill explained. "It is an official enquiry into the cause of death."

"But," Stroganoff objected, "for what purpose? We know already that Anton is shot."

"In spite of that your presence will be necessary."

"*Mais, mon ami, ca ne m'amuse pas*," said Stroganoff. "And besides this I am too busy. Every Friday morning I work with Stanley on my autobiography."

"I will buy a copy," Quill promised.

"I give you one for nothing. Signed."

"Thanks " said Quill. "But I'm afraid you must attend the inquest just the same. It won't take long and anyway they will pay you for it."

"Poof," said Stroganoff, "the money it interests me not. I am an artist. How much?"

Quill temporised and succeeded in leaving Stroganoff under the impression that he was coming into a small fortune.

"Me," he beamed affluently at Quill, "I have the theory. I tell you. To-day when I lunch I begin suddenly to think. Who, I ask myself, would want to kill Palook? Everybody, I answer. But who would want to kill him especially, I continue. Well, there is still many people. There is even myself. I do all for Palook. I make him star, I gave him best dressing-room, I lend him money, and all he say is contract, contract, contract. But me, I do not suspect myself, so I knew it must be somebody else."

Quill suppressed a smile. "I follow your reasoning," he said gravely.

"It is clear—no?" said Stroganoff delighted. "Then I ask myself—is it M'sieur Saintly? No. Arenskaya? No. Puthyk? No. Kasha, Pavel, Nevajno? No. The *corps de ballet?* No. They work too hard. Stanley—per'aps, but I think he is too stupid. He would miss. The little Rubinska? No. But the mother of Rubinska! Ah, I tell myself, here is a different colour of a cow."

"Horse," corrected Quill.

"Horse," agreed Stroganoff affably. "That mother I put nothing past her. She is awful woman—the daughter of a dog, *une femme formidable*. First she want a contract for seven years for her daughter, then she want no contract, only more money. Then she want all the best roles, and then to please her I must sack my Shura who dance so nice. Our assassin—*assurément* she is him."

"And your reasons for this view?"

"You English you always want reasons," said Stroganoff irritably. "For me it is enough that I suspect."

"But what makes you suspect?" Quill persevered. So far the story sounded like mere personal animosity, but there might be something behind it.

Stroganoff sought a sulky refuge in his tea. Then suddenly he brightened as one to whom light has been vouchsafed.

"Yesterday," he said, "she came to me before the performance and ask to borrow my revolver. She always ask for something, so I lent it her and think nothing of it."

This was altogether incredible. Quill said as much. Stroganoff persisted weakly, but eventually gave way.

"Oh, all right," he admitted cheerfully. "That I invent. But now I tell you the truth."

"And mind it is the truth," said Quill. With another man he would have delivered a severe censure on the enormity of attempting to mislead Scotland Yard, but with this particular witness it would clearly be a waste of time.

"The truth," said Stroganoff solemnly. "It is you will understand *la scandale*, so you must not repeat. You will be discreet—no?" And with many gestures he launched into the story.

"Until last year," he began, "the little Rubinska she dance the Swan Queen *comme une petite vierge*. No good. Often I tell her so. My child, I tell her, *mais gentilment*, you must take for yourself a lover. And I select for her many estimable young men. But always she refuse. These English girls they are so respectable. And then suddenly I notice she dance right. So I enquire. And to my disgust it is Anton. Alas, I say, that is bad. *Une mauvaise affaire*. Anton will tire soon and—poof— off he go."

So, Stroganoff went on, he had gone to warn her mother. Quill gathered that it had been a difficult interview. Stroganoff in his innocence had assumed that the mother knew all about the affair and, unaware of Palook's true character, probably approved of it as likely to help her daughter's career. It had taken a long time to convince the mother that her daughter was no longer a virgin, and then she muddled the issue by insisting upon marriage. Stroganoff had not been able to move her from that view. If the villain would not marry her daughter, she said, she would strangle him with her own hands.

"But she shoot him instead," said Stroganoff happily and leant back in his chair with an air of triumph.

But this man who had never seen *Petroushka* seemed singularly hard to convince. He kept on worrying about the mother's opportunity to fire. Was she anywhere near the stage, he asked, which was stupid, as everybody knew that woman was always near the stage when her daughter danced. "Other mothers they obey, but this one never. Besides she have a part in *Petroushka* and stand on the balcony to wave a scarf. Only this time," he ended triumphantly, "she wave a pistol."

"Then she was on the balcony that night."

"*Mais naturellement*," said Stroganoff, "I tell you . . ."

What he was about to tell remained a mystery for at that moment the door was flung open and a large disgruntled tornado burst into the room. A smaller tornado followed.

The large tornado circled the room and came furiously to rest in front of Stroganoff's desk, where it solidified into the formidable outlines of Madame Rubinska and demanded:

"Is it correct that you have decided to give Anton's dressing-room to that man?"

"Which man?" said Stroganoff playing for time.

"Pavel," put in the small tornado who in repose appeared as a dark, tired wisp of a girl. She had the soft voice of a dancer and a dancer's large expressive eyes. Her mouth was also large, but this she inherited from her mother.

"Pavel," echoed the large tornado. "Pavel!" And the concrete walls quivered beneath the noxious syllables.

"I do not give him," said Stroganoff craftily, "I only lend him."

"That's a lie," said the tornado briskly, "and you know it. They're nailing up his mascots there now."

Stroganoff looked at Quill, and found his expression a mixture of sympathy and awe, but no admiration. It seemed to give him courage.

"All right," he said defiantly. "It is a lie. I give it to Pavel. So what you do now?"

"I'll tell you what I'll do," said the tornado. "I'll tell you what I'll do . . ." she thought furiously.

"Maybe," asked the ever-hopeful Stroganoff, "you like your contract back—no?"

"Exactly," said the tornado. "Unless that flying fish goes out of the dressing-room to-night, I go to Buttonhooke to-morrow."

"Alone?" asked the optimist.

"With my daughter. She shall not dance for you again."

"Poof!"

"Further, she shall not dance for you to-night."

This shook Stroganoff, but not nearly as badly as it shook Rubinska. It was to be her first London appearance in *Lac des Cygnes* since her celebrated deflowering, her first chance to confound the critics who last year had markedly admired nothing but her technique. And here was Momma getting impulsive again.

"Aren't we being rather hasty, Mother," she put in.

A hurt and dazed tornado flopped into an armchair. Quill felt that had she but known the expression, she would have said "*Et tu Brute.*"

"After all," continued Rubinska, "Pavel is a star and we don't want to upset him. Besides, his lifts are magnificent."

"*Epatant*," agreed Stroganoff, rallying to this unexpected ally.

"Lifts," soughed the tornado. "You have been ignored, insulted, pushed aside for the benefit of a man who looks like a lounge lizard, and dances like a policeman, and all you can do is rant about his lifts."

"They are important," said Stroganoff critically. "Not so important as elevation. . . ."

"And not so important as that matter of the dressing-room."

"A good elevation," pursued Stroganoff, wrapped in his own eloquence, "it is a quarter of the combat. The other three-quarters it is the management." He bowed tactlessly at the tornado. "A good management," he added quickly, "it is like a mother to a dancer. It pushes, it praises, and it is always by her side."

"If," said the tornado grimly, "you imagine you can flatter me into forgetting my daughter's interests for a moment, you are wrong. That dressing-room. . . ."

"We do not discuss that now," said Stroganoff magnificently, if a trifle late. "It is not important. What is important is that my company are good comrades, that we work together, that we turn over every stone, that we all one happy family—until Wednesday week. Your daughter then must dance the doll before Benois himself—if he comes. And if he do not come we do not tell the papers, so the effect it is the same. So how can you think of dressing-rooms at such moments? Besides," he added, "I just decided not to give it to anybody. I give it to our friend here to help him find our assassin." He waved a baleful hand at Quill. "He is from the police and very quick to catch assassins," he said meaningly. "Soon he will ask you many questions *bien embarrassant*."

"I will not have my daughter worried on the evening of a performance," declared the tornado glaring at Quill defiantly. "She must have calm and rest. After the show we'll have to put up with you, but not now. Come, darling."

She flounced out of her chair, easily evaded Stroganoff's gallant attempt to kiss her hand, and sailed out. The daughter followed obediently.

* * * * *

"Poof," said Stroganoff, uneasily.

"Poof," agreed Quill.

"Now that you have seen her," said Stroganoff, "you are convinced that she is the assassin—no?"

Quill regretted that he was, as yet, not persuaded and resumed the discussion that the mother had interrupted.

"You said she was on the balcony that night."

"Sure," said Stroganoff, "I see her myself."

"Then you were in the wings?"

Stroganoff shrugged. "Sometimes in the wings, sometimes in the box, sometimes I talk to the critics. Me I am everywhere."

"But where exactly were you at the time of the murder?"

Stroganoff shifted uneasily.

"Poof," he said, "that does not matter."

Quill said it did matter. Stroganoff pleaded that it was personal business and nothing to do with the crime. Quill insisted. It was merely a matter of routine, he stressed, but he had to get these things right.

Thus pressed, Stroganoff admitted reluctantly that he had been involved in some slight unpleasantness. He was in his box during the fatal act watching the performance, when suddenly he noticed someone on the right-hand balcony who had no right to be there.

"An impostor," he said indignantly. "An impersonator. So me I run to the wings, borrow the Arabian dressing-gown and climb up to catch him blue-handed. But I am too slow and when I arrive he already invisible. So I come down and then Anton is dead and I am too busy since to tick him off. But I do it now." He rang a bell. Nothing happened.

"Did you see anybody on the balcony when you were up there?" asked Quill.

"But there were many people," said Stroganoff. "Only they all coming down—but I push and look only for one man. But it is evident that he come down before I arrive."

"And this man you were looking for—who is he?"

"That," said Stroganoff, "is a matter for the Ballets Stroganoff only."

"In a case of murder it is also the business of the police. I must insist on his name."

"Me—I forget it," said Stroganoff evasively. "It is difficult to remember all these long Russian names—no?" he added hopefully.

However, Quill was not to be put off. For five minutes Stroganoff wriggled, prevaricated, dived into and was jerked back from many fascinating byways. After which time, exhausted, his memory returned. Reluctantly he yielded the name.

It was that of Pavel's dresser—Serge Appelsinne.

CHAPTER VII

It was just after 4 p.m. that Quill left Stroganoff's office and made his way to the stage-doorkeeper's room, where instinct told him he would find his assistant, Sergeant Banner. The sergeant, he felt, could well relieve him of the next step in the case—the checking up of the contradictory statements made

by Stroganoff and Serge Appelsinne. Stroganoff claimed to
have seen Appelsinne on the balcony. Appelsinne's statement
was that he had been standing in the wings with Pavel's
dressing-gown and subsequently talked to Pavel. With the
numerous witnesses available for interrogation, Quill felt that
it ought not to be difficult for the sergeant to discover which
of these statements was correct. If it could be proved that
Appelsinne had been on that balcony—well, the latter would
have to do a lot of explaining.

His instinct had not misled him. The sergeant was sitting in
front of the fire, drinking tea—English tea—listening en-
raptured to the stage-doorkeeper's lurid, and in most cases
slanderous, recollections of life behind the scenes.

" 'Noel,' I says to him, 'Noel,' I says, 'you're wasting your
time,' " the latter was orating. " 'She won't look at you.' But
would he listen to me?"

Quill would not have minded listening himself, but the
dignity of the Yard would hardly permit it. He beckoned the
reluctant sergeant outside, presented him with Stanley's list of
the occupants of the balconies and gave his instructions.

"Leave it to me," said Sergeant Banner importantly. "I'll
make them talk."

"They'll talk all right," smiled Quill. "Your trouble will be
to make them keep to the point."

Curiously complacent at having thus neatly saddled Banner
with part of his own sufferings, and pondering happily whether
the reactions of the sergeant to the company would be stronger
than the reactions of the company to the sergeant, Quill took
a taxi to the hotel to interview the Puthyks. In spite of the
exciting contradictions which Banner was now perspiringly
investigating, he had no intention of neglecting any alternative
avenues, however remote. Both Appelsinne and Stroganoff
might turn out to be lying, but it did not follow from this that
either was necessarily guilty of the murder. (To travel
cautiously is better than to fall down—Detective's Handbook,

Rule 27.) To remind him of this there was the awful example of his last case; a small matter of destruction by fire of a block of service flats, a restaurant and bridge club, the owner of which not only possessed a heavy overdraft, no tenants, and an insurance policy due to lapse the following week, but had been observed just before the outbreak, fondling a tin of petrol. In spite of the fellow's protests that his car had run dry some quarter of a mile away, he was arrested, only to prove at the trial—in a defence meanly reserved—that he had been speaking the truth and that the fire was caused by a commonplace gas leak. Subsequently he sued the police for wrongful arrest and cleaned up a packet—all of which made things no easier for Quill. So he was jumping to no conclusions now, however tempting they might be.

The Puthyks occupied a double bedroom on the fifth floor. Quill's luck was in for Arenskaya was out. Amid the wildly congested acreage of five cabin trunks, seven hat-boxes, a fleet of attache cases and Puthyk's cabinet, the old man was enjoying a doze. He yawned vaguely at Quill's entry.

"We pay the bill next week," he promised and turned over. It seemed almost a shame to disturb him, but Quill patted him on the back and thrust his official card into his hand. It blinked Puthyk into wakefulness. He jumped from the bed and exuded hospitality.

"Wiskyansoda?" he asked.

But there was none.

"Cigar?"

The cabinet was empty.

Quill offered his cigarette case. Puthyk accepted happily.

Quill followed with his subpœna. The old man, not understanding, seemed delighted.

"I will make you tea," he promised. "Russian tea with lemon." Before Quill could stop him, he had bustled to a trunk, thrown out a dusty file, a number of ballet shoes and an old pair of corsets, and triumphantly produced a dilapidated kettle, a rickety spirit stove, and an evil-looking lemon. Then he busied himself with the sheer mechanics of the problem. After this Quill could not very well refuse the yellow concoction that was beamingly handed to him.

While the kettle had been boiling, Puthyk had kept up a continuous stream of babble, drifting from subject to subject, but concentrating mainly on a eulogy of his own performance in *Petroushka* that morning. The ritual of tea-drinking, however, while not reducing him to silence, at least made him pause long enough to swallow, which enabled Quill to get in his little speech about a routine interrogation.

"I understand," he said, "that you were among those that occupied the right-hand balcony during the performance."

The old man blushed and bowed his head. "It is true," he admitted. "I—Puthyk—premier ballerin of the Maryinsky, who have danced before the Tsar, the Kaiser and many presidents, and received their congratulations, now walk on to the balcony. But what would you? One must live—and they say I am too old to dance. But they are wrong," he said more loudly. "My legs are a little tired, maybe, but my technique and my *caractère*, they are still unequalled. Did I not prove it to them this morning?"

"You certainly did," Quill consoled him.

"Ah," said Puthyk sorrowfully, "you understand. You are an artist. But the others, they are not convinced. Nevertheless, I will convince them. You will see."

"Of course you will," Quill agreed. "But when you were on the balcony did you notice anybody or anything that struck you as in any way unusual?"

The old man pondered.

"I notice that Anton he dance disgusting. But that is not unusual. He always dance disgusting. When I remember the Petroushkas that have been—Nijinsky, Bolm, Woizikovsky—myself—and then Anton Palook—well—my blood it simmer like a samovar."

With some difficulty Quill managed to dislodge him from the subject of Palook's inferior technique.

"I have been informed," he said, "that you and Palook were not on the best of terms."

"It is a lie," said the old man indignantly. "We never speak to each other."

"And why was that?"

Puthyk shrugged. "*Il est peu intéressant.* He was just what you say—a conceiter. We have nothing in common."

"Your wife found him interesting."

"My wife," said Puthyk, "think as I do. She always afraid he drop the ballerina. But he only do it once—in *Aurore*. It was Durakova and the things she say to him afterwards!" The old man slapped his knee and laughed heartily at the memory. "Anton explain later that he was sozzled, but for a dancer that is no excuse."

Once again Quill felt that they were drifting from the point.

"Still," he said, "your wife thought more of him as a man than as a dancer."

"But no," he said. "It is ten years since she slept with him."

"And you have forgotten and forgiven?"

"Forgotten?" said Puthyk. "No. I never forget that."

Quill waited.

"My wife and I," said Puthyk, "we often laugh at it still. You see," he added confidentially, "Anton very bad in bed. Now when I was a young man I . . ."

Quill staunched the reminiscence just in time. He was beginning to realise that as a jealous husband Puthyk hardly came up to scratch. He turned the conversation to Puthyk's movements on the balcony, but here the old man was vagueness itself, and even showed a tendency to get huffy at what he clearly considered Quill's tactlessness in concentrating on his present lowly status as a dancer. He was just reminding Quill of his triumph in Paris, when the door opened to admit a large cabbage, a bouquet of roses, a box of Turkish delight, a portable gramophone and a shrill stream of Russian. Behind them was Arenskaya.

"Ah," she beamed at Quill. "M'sieu le detective. Wiskyan-soda?"

This was too much for Quill. He collapsed weakly in a chair.

"There is no whisky," explained Puthyk.

"Then we make him Russian tea."

"I have done so," said Puthyk with dignity.

"It matters nothing," said Arenskaya. "We make some more." She grinned wickedly at Quill. "So you come to see me already? You are, what they call, a quick worker!"

"You make the mistake," said Puthyk. "He come to see me and soon I give him my autograph."

"But no," contradicted Arenskaya, pityingly. "He does not come to see you. You just here. It is evident he come for me. He try to make the *rendezvous* this morning. So now you must go away and leave us."

Quill rose hurriedly. He could not be really certain that Arenskaya meant what she seemed to be meaning, but he was taking no chances.

"I will see you at the theatre to-night," he said and fled.

"He is in a hurry that one—no?" said Puthyk wonderingly.

* * * * *

Back to the theatre to find a purple-faced Sergeant Banner clamouring for the arrest of a young exquisite who had amiably mistaken the Sergeant's shy approach for a suggestion of quite a different character. To the pub, to repair the Sergeant's self-respect and send him back to an enquiry he threatened to abandon. Back to Earl's Court, to evade Miss Treacle and find a boiled shirt, a tepid meal, and the theatre again. Straight into Stroganoff's welcoming arms.

"You have never seen *Lac des Cygnes*—no?" beamed the latter, grasped him by the arm, planted him inescapably in his box, and told him to keep quiet.

The curtain was going up.

CHAPTER VIII

As to the presentation of *Lac des Cygnes*, there are two schools of thought.

School One presents the ballet in four irrelevant acts. In addition it supplies a fleet of cardboard ducks and trails them triumphantly across the painted waters of the back-cloth, to well-timed gasps of admiration. School Two abolishes the birds and admiration, and stops short only of abolishing the entire ballet, condensing it into a single act, which sends the unseasoned ballet-goer away with the unfortunate impression that the hero has been left alive after all.

Stroganoff, with great resource, combined both methods. He gave the ballet in one act, but inserted all the more formidable features of the other three. He reduced the pictured lake to the dimensions of a puddle, but rolled on a couple of tipsy-looking turkeys. Puthyk proudly collected these masterpieces of carpentry as they arrived in the wings and trundled them round the back, ready for despatch upon another voyage at the end of the ballet.

To-night the birds were tired and stopped half way across.

A body of pudding-faces, wearing bi-coloured leotards and Glyndebourne hats came hurrying on to the stage. The birds ignored them. The huntsmen strode about, making tallyho gestures with their wooden hunting bows and cursing the turkeys under their breath. They were led by a fair, slim dancer, alert and really interested in what he was doing. Quill recognized Kasha Ranevsky.

To them, revolting in purple and primrose, Pavel, the Prince. He paused to receive some scattered applause. Not so the conductor. Volti-Subito had no intention of allowing his "boys" to lose their places while that purple petunia stood and smirked at the gallery. He worked up a smart *accelerando* that sent the huntsmen hareing off and brought on the Swan Queen at the double. Now, however, he relented, for he liked the little Rubinska.

Dressed in the foam of a white tu-tu, a crown of brilliants upon her sleek hair, her slender legs taut, and tapering to a pink satin ballet-shoe, and all about her a shimmer of brilliants —drops of clear water that she had not shaken from her plumes—the Swan Queen preened herself. Changed by the enchantments of a wizard into a swan, she could emerge only in this hour of blue limes, white spots, surprise pinks and no amber. What the Emperor Concerto is to the pianist, what Juliet is to the actress, what the triple squeeze position is to the bridge player, is the Swan Queen to the dancer.

Rubinska's Swan Queen was more bird than ballerina. There was something very tentative about this swan. The tough and tried old Swans in the *corps de ballet* made this fledgling seem the more touching for their air of rather tired experience.

Pavel was a raddled prince. The lines of his role had, as it were, grown on him. He stalked the stage with a certain weary grace, and though, in the *pas-de-deux* that followed, his eyes were on the ballerina, his hands ready to catch and lift her, it was all a matter of habit.

To see Pavel was not, as a rule, to love him. In fact their first meeting had had the very reverse effect upon Quill. But here, in the ballet, everything was different. The Swan Queen saw him—loved him.

There follows a passage of expressive mime, in which Rubinska flaps her arms to show that she is a swan—besides she is dressed in feathers. Pavel looks sadly at his wooden bow and carefully shakes his head. Together they wander off presumably for some more of this animated conversation. On troop the swans. They run about flapping their arms and arching their necks. No doubt they mean well. Lines, never the strong point of the Ballets Stroganoff, were always at their most wavering in *Lac des Cygnes*.

"My company they are artists—they wish always to express themselves, and you cannot," explained Stroganoff urgently, "express yourself in a straight line. Arenskaya, she curses, but me I say 'Poof,' and afterwards I fine them."

At the end of the dance the swans wedge themselves neatly in the corner of the stage, while the pudding-faces wander back, and aim their wooden bows at them. To them Pavel. He was about to reason with them and beg them to spare the swans with a great deal of romantic arm work, when the insubordinate turkeys, heretofore sentient, began bucking like bronchos. Rubinska, running on to stand in front of the *corps de ballet*, protecting them with her own slim arms, bit back her laughter. This was her big chance to show all London, and her mother, what she could do with the role. She caught sight of Kasha, and took heart.

Kasha Ranevsky wore his role with a difference. Here, you felt, would one day be a Prince to match the wondering quality of Rubinska's Swan. Indeed, the ballet reached the high point of its achievement in the difficult lift in the grand *adageo* that followed, when the ballerina, having danced with her Prince, is caught, as she falls to the stage, and lies tautly across the arm of the second cavalier. Kasha looked down at Rubinska. Rubinska looked up at Kasha. Even Quill felt at that moment that something had been born.

After this the *pas-de-quatre* for the cygnets. A certain amount of hooting and tooting from Volti-Subito's "boys" heralded on the four shortest, but not necessarily youngest, members of the company.

"My orchestra, it plays well, no?" observed Stroganoff complacently.

The cygnets linked arms and began one of the most famous dances in the ballet.

"*Magnifique*," said Stroganoff.

But the tough appearance of the four seasoned ducks that made up the *pas-de-quatre* in the Ballets Stroganoff was altogether too much for Quill. . . . He excused himself.

"The door at the bottom of the passage," waved Stroganoff absently, wrapt in his contemplation of the stage.

In the wings the confusion was reasonable. This means that it was not so bad as it might have been, but still worse than anything that Quill had visualized. Since the entire *corps de ballet* was at this moment disporting itself on the stage, in a patch of undisciplined beauty that was at once the delight of Stroganoff and despair of Arenskaya, only the principals were in the wings. There was, of course, the usual whiskered foam of generals that surround even the minor activities of ballet. There were also several vigilant dressers, several even more vigilant mothers, several hampered stage hands, a livid stage manager and his fumble-fisted assistant. There was Arenskaya making rude remarks about the fat girl, and the fat girl's mother carefully failing to hear them. There was Puthyk, bent double over the contraption of pulleys that worked the turkeys, imperiously waving off the stage carpenter whose job it was, and Stanley, to whom anything mechanical held an irresistible appeal. There was Sergeant Banner, once again fascinated, sitting on a piece of scenery that would shortly be required, and there was Rubinska.

She was tapping a satin shoe, testing the block before the cascade of *échappés* that she was due to perform with the ease of an angel and the toes of a martyr, while beside her, on guard, stood the mother dragon, her eyes defying young Kasha Ranevsky, standing hopefully a few yards away, to come any nearer. Quill, who fancied himself as a psychologist, strolled over and congratulated her on her performance.

"It was better?" asked Rubinska. "Warmer?"

"Great," said Quill. "Even greater than your doll this morning."

"Ah, this morning, I could not dance," sighed Rubinska. "I was sad."

Quill nodded. "You were very friendly with Palook."

"I was his mistress," said Rubinska simply.

But the mother rushed in to defend her child's honour.

"Of course," she said, "they were engaged."

"That is a lie," said Rubinska wearily. "We were not engaged. In fact our affair was over, as everybody in the company has no doubt already informed the Inspector."

"Well!" gasped the mother. It was a new experience to have her daughter defying her, and one she felt curiously incapable of handling. She backed away like a defeated steam-roller. "You will find me in your dressing-room when you have recovered your senses," she snapped.

Rubinska smiled at Quill. "Poor mother, she can't get used to it." Then suddenly, as though jerked by a string, she left Quill's side and sped on to the stage.

The fascinated Sergeant Banner rose and crossed over to Quill.

"I'm getting on better," he confided. "Have all you want by the morning. An' it seems to me that most of the blokes you saw this morning was liars."

Quill was interested. "You've found out something?"

"Plenty," said the Sergeant. "But I'm not through yet. Several other people I gotter see. As a matter of fact," said the Sergeant unexpectedly, "I'm taking one of them to supper. That one." He pointed to the fat girl.

"Sergeant!" said Quill, shocked.

"It's only in the course of my duty," said Sergeant Banner solemnly. "You told me to ask questions, didn't you? And all women talk better over steak and chips." He strolled importantly away and then ruined his effect by turning round and winking.

Rubinska was back in the wings. Then she was on the stage again taking curtain after curtain. Now she was

C

surrounded by a crowd babbling congratulations. It was some time before Quill could get at her.

"I'm having supper with Kasha," she told him in response to his request for an interview, "but if you like, you can come and talk to me in my dressing-room while I'm changing."

"Your mother?" said Quill.

"I'll get rid of mother," promised Rubinska. "I'm sick of mother."

She was as good as her word. Quill, waiting in the corridor, heard an explosion of angry sentences and then the dragon emerged, slammed the door, blasted Quill with a look, and trundled dazedly off.

Quill knocked and entered. Rubinska, at her dressing-table, looked at him mischievously.

"That's the first time I've ever stood up to mother," she confided, "and it's surprising how easy it is once you start." She paused. "Now, what is it you would like to know?"

Quill delivered his usual speech. Rubinska nodded.

"You are hoping that, as Anton's mistress, I might have something interesting to tell you. But I'm afraid you'll be disappointed. I doubt if I can tell you anything you haven't already heard from the others. And I was in my dressing-room at the time of the shot, so I didn't even see anything that might prove useful."

"Does that mean," asked Quill, "that you didn't take your curtains?" He had been revolving in the ballet world long enough by now to realize that this was almost incredible. But Rubinska nodded.

"It's unheard of, I know, but I went straight to my dressing-room after leaving the stage. Kasha Ranevsky escorted me, so he can bear me out. And then Arenskaya came and found me."

Quill remembered something "She found you crying."

"So she's told you," said Rubinska. "Yes, I was crying."

"Because Palook was dead?"

"I didn't know he was dead," said Rubinska, and for no reason that he could discover, Quill believed her. "No—I was crying because something that happened during the performance upset me. That's why I didn't stop for my curtains."

Quill smoked thoughtfully.

"I don't want to seem tactless," he said at length, "but could you tell me what it was that upset you?"

"It was nothing to do with the murder."

"Very probably not," Quill admitted. "But one never knows in these cases—and I can't afford to take any chances. Should it prove irrelevant I promise you that anything you say will be treated as strictly confidential."

"But it was nothing," said Rubinska. "Just that Anton and I had a quarrel during the performance."

"During?"

"You know the booths that house the puppets at the back of the stage. Well, my booth is next to Anton's and the walls are very thin." She swallowed. "Well—I know a girl is supposed to have her pride and all that but," she swallowed again, "it was the first time that I've found myself anything like alone with Anton for over a month—he's taken care of that—and I couldn't resist an appeal to him. I started it in the first scene and he wasn't too unkind. Not that he said anything definite but he called me *malenkaia dyrotchka*—that means 'little fool'—and that was always his favourite form of endearment."

"One moment," interposed Quill. "The booth on the other side of you, if I remember rightly, is occupied by Pavel. Do you think he could overhear your conversation?"

Rubinska actually laughed. "He could and did. But—believe it or not—I'd forgotten all about him and his jealousy until I saw his eyes in the middle of our *pas-de-deux*. The hate in them was positively terrifying. It's no wonder Arenskaya says I danced badly last night. I defy anyone to dance well with a partner they feel wants to murder them. I've heard since that Anton and Pavel had a terrific row in the interval."

"About you?"

"About me. But I didn't hear about it till much later. That's why, when I was back in the booth in the last act, I spoke to Anton again. And this time he wasn't so kind. In fact he was just beastly." And to Quill's horror and embarrassment, her eyes filled with tears.

Palook, she went on to tell him, had exploded at her first words. He had said that he was sick to death of being pestered by jealous women—or men for that matter—that when he was through he was through. An artist who lived on his emotions never went back to an old love—of either sex— and to-night he was going to accept the invitation of a society woman, who would be too scared of her reputation to make a fuss when he had tired. Couldn't Pavel and she console each other and leave him alone? And he had not bothered to lower his voice throughout—Rubinska thought he wanted to make certain that Pavel should hear him.

"But it wasn't only Pavel who heard. Kasha Ranevsky, I think, heard too, though he never said anything. But he was waiting for me when I came off and he escorted me to my dressing-room without making any comment, and left me alone to cry. He's a dear boy," added Rubinska irrelevantly.

There was just one other point to be cleared up.

"And when did you learn that Palook had been shot?"

Rubinska said it was shortly after Arenskaya had left her. Her mother had told her.

"It's curious," said Quill bluntly. "Arenskaya said you told her."

Rubinska seemed surprised. "We hardly spoke at all. She came bursting into the room, I imagine to curse me for my dancing, and found me crying. She asked me what was up, and I said, 'Anton.' And she gave a yelp and literally raced out of the room." She turned to Quill. "Do you think I looked so tragic that she thought I meant Anton was dead?"

"Anything is possible with these Russians," said Quill tactfully.

As a matter of precaution he had a few words with Arenskaya before leaving the theatre. Her version tallied with Rubinska's.

"Naturally," she said, "I know something happen to Anton when he do not take his curtains. And then I find Rubinska cry and shout his name. And I know at once that something terrible has happen. He is dead, I think, and I go to see. And was I not right?"

She also added that she had witnessed the quarrel between Pavel and Palook, but such things were *trop ordinaire* to interest her.

CHAPTER IX

A HIGHLY complacent Sergeant Banner greeted Quill on his arrival at the Yard the following morning. Listening to his exploits, Quill had to admit that this complacency was to a large extent justified. The Sergeant might not, as he proudly claimed, have solved the mystery, but his researches had certainly revealed some startling facts. His report, which he insisted on elaborating with some quite interesting but entirely irrelevant personal adventures, may, in its essentials, be summarized as follows:

Stroganoff had told the truth. Several people had seen him going up on the balcony, several people had seen him on it, and a carpenter and two members of the *corps de ballet* had noticed him coming down a few seconds before Palook was shot. Stroganoff, therefore, was not the murderer.

Appelsinne had lied. He was on the balcony, dressed in

a peasant's costume, exactly as Stroganoff had stated. Several
of the cast had noticed him. However, he had descended
before Stroganoff had arrived (this also was vouched for)
and was standing in the wings when Palook was shot.
(Vouched for again.) Therefore, he, too, was not the murderer.
Nevertheless he had thought it necessary to lie to Quill.
Why?

The answer, it emerged, was Pavel. Pavel and Appelsinne
had provided each other with an alibi. But Pavel had not
been in the wings as he claimed. He had been on the balcony.
The same three witnesses who had seen Stroganoff had seen
Pavel, on leaving the stage, sprint round and climb up on
the balcony, arriving as the cast on the balcony were preparing
to go down, and standing in the rear, near the doorway,
where he could not be seen from the front.   Several of the
cast had noticed him in his Moor's costume as they brushed
past. One of them had even noticed Pavel beckoning urgently
to Appelsinne, who had come over and after a few words
handed over something—they could not say what. Curiously
enough no one had seen Pavel come down, though the
carpenter thought he had caught a glimpse of him at the
bottom of the balcony stairs and making for the curtain a few
seconds after it had been rung down—that is, a few seconds
after Palook had been shot. He had appeared in front of the
curtain to make his bow to the audience, as he had stated.
He had, however, been one of the last players to do so.

Thinking over the evidence, Quill decided that it was
quite possible for Pavel to have done the murder. He had
the motive—jealousy—and now it was proved that he also
had the opportunity. As shown in the statement he was
on the balcony at the critical moment and the time between
the shot and Pavel's appearance in front of the audience was
just about long enough for Pavel to leave the balcony and
dash round before the curtain. This was also consistent with
his rather belated appearance.

As for means, it had only to be proved that Pavel possessed, or had access to, a revolver—and the case was almost complete.

A sudden thought struck Quill. Stroganoff. Stroganoff had gone up to that balcony to look for Appelsinne. He had not found Appelsinne. But he must in that case have seen Pavel. Why had he not mentioned it? He could not have overlooked him. A lesser member Stroganoff might not have noticed—but Pavel in the Moor's make-up and costume must have leapt to the eye—especially as he had no right to be there. And Stroganoff had already amply demonstrated his capacity for spotting people who were where they had no right to be.

Quill determined to tackle Stroganoff about this and found himself wondering how the wily Russian would explain it away. That he would not be at a loss for an explanation Quill was certain.

With three liars to interview, Quill was in some doubt as to which liar to approach first. Eventually he decided that he would start with Appelsinne, if only because he seemed a little less glib than the other two. Realizing that it was essential to see Appelsinne alone, Quill arrived at the theatre at eleven o'clock, when Pavel was pretty certain to be in class. To make sure, he looked in at the practise room on his way up.

"When I say ta-ra-ra," Arenskaya was shrilling, "why do you play ti-ta-ta-tum?" The pianist snorted and banged down the loud pedal.

Everything was evidently quite normal. Quill noted Pavel in a corner doing the *barre* a favour and, satisfied, went on his way.

But a pop-eyed Stanley materialized in the corner and grasped him urgently by the arm.

"I've found something frightfully important," he panted.

"Later," said Quill, only just resisting borrowing the Stroganoff formula of "Go away."

"You'll never guess what it is," said Stanley, oblivious.

"Another button?"

"Better than that." Stanley glanced round mysteriously. "I've found it."

"What?"

"This." Stanley delved into his pockets and produced a bulky shape rolled in a handkerchief. Quill unrolled it. It was a revolver.

Quill experienced the emotion felt by the celebrated Inspector French at least a dozen times in every volume. That is to say he was delighted. He examined his capture gloatingly while Stanley stood by awaiting the applause.

It was an ordinary service revolver—of the same calibre that had killed Palook. One bullet had been fired from the chamber. It was doubtless the murderer's gun.

"Good boy," said Quill approvingly. "You remembered not to touch it."

"Well—I did touch it at first in my excitement at finding it," admitted Stanley reluctantly. "But I only touched it a little."

"And where did you find it?" asked Quill. If only he had found it in Pavel's quarters.

He had. In the waste-paper basket—of all places.

"After everybody had gone yesterday," explained Stanley, "I decided to search all the rooms."

"Why?" asked Quill. "The police searched the place pretty thoroughly on the night of the murder."

"You never know," said Stanley. "Thought I might find something useful. And didn't I?"

This was undeniable.

"I found a lot of queer things," said Stanley, blushing slightly at the recollection, "but none of them seemed relevant. And then I came to Pavel's old dressing-room. He moved to Palook's room last night, you know. Well, I said to myself, people often leave valuable evidence behind when they move."

But hardly, thought Quill, a gun with which they have committed a murder.

"Well," said Stanley, "the place was a mess. But I went over it thoroughly. And then I noticed the waste-paper basket which was full of telegrams, letters, empty tins, dead flowers and so on. So I thought I might as well look through that. And there half-way down was the revolver. And now," he finished eagerly, "I suppose you're going to arrest Pavel."

Quill laughed. "It isn't as simple as that. There is no evidence at all that it is Pavel's revolver or that he put it there. And in any case it could not have been there when the police searched. It may have been planted there later. I suppose quite a lot of people go in and out of Pavel's quarters during the day?"

"Plenty," said Stanley downcast. But soon he brightened again. "Shall I get you a list of all the people that have been in Pavel's rooms since the murder?"

Quill imagined the list would comprise the entire company, but it was as good a method of getting rid of Stanley as any other.

"Do," he said cordially.

With an important nod, Stanley went off on his task and Quill reached Pavel's dressing-room without further interruption.

Appelsinne, in his new quarters, was busily ironing a costume in which, in due course, Pavel would no doubt appear revolting. He did not look at all pleased to see Quill. He did not even offer him Russian tea.

"My master is in class," he said curtly, and went on ironing.

"Direct attack is best with sulky suspects." (Detective's Handbook, Rule 57.)

Quill came to the point at once.

"Why," he asked, "did you lie to me yesterday?"

Appelsinne regarded him warily, but said nothing.

"You told me that at the end of *Petroushka* you were waiting in the wings."

"Yes."

"With Pavel."

"Yes."

"Actually," said Quill, "you were up on the right-hand balcony wearing a peasant's costume."

"It is a lie."

"I have half a dozen people who saw you."

Appelsinne put down his iron, picked up the dress and hung it carefully in the wardrobe. Then he returned and faced Quill.

"It is true I was up there," he admitted. "What of that?"

"Only," said Quill gently, "that this is a case of murder. There may be nothing wrong in your being on the balcony, but it is very serious when you lie to me about it."

Appelsinne sulked.

"I was up there to get a better view of the dancing."

"Why did you not tell me this before?"

Appelsinne smiled. "That is simple. It is against the rules that I go up, also I had to borrow the costume, and I feared that you would tell all this to Stroganoff and then he fire me."

"But some of the company who saw you might have told Stroganoff."

"No."

"Actually, Stroganoff himself saw you."

"I know," said Appelsinne wearily. "He told me."

"But why," asked Quill, "run such risks merely for a better view of *Petroushka?*"

"It is my favourite ballet," said Appelsinne defiantly.

"I suggest," said Quill, "that you were on the balcony for an entirely different reason."

"No."

"You were up there to shoot Palook." And quite suddenly

Quill felt that he had hit on the truth. Appelsinne was furiously jealous of Palook. He had gone up on the balcony to shoot him. Stroganoff had seen him there. So had Pavel. Stroganoff had gone round to curse. Pavel, divining his intention, to stop him. Pavel had got there first, taken his gun (here was the object that was seen being passed) and sent Appelsinne away. And then Pavel, who'd just had a row with Palook, had yielded to sudden opportunity and shot him. It was all pure theory, of course, but it fitted the facts.

Appelsinne's reactions, too, confirmed it. As far as it was possible for such a swarthy skin, he had turned pale.

"No," he said.

"You were jealous of Palook."

"No. Yes. I was jealous. All the world know I am jealous." Appelsinne was rapidly losing control. "Many times I could shoot with pleasure." He recovered himself. "But nevertheless I did not shoot him. I was not on the balcony when Palook die. I was in the wings. There will be people who see me."

"That's all right," said Quill. "I never said you shot him. I know you were not on the balcony by that time. I only said you went up there to shoot him. And you admit that—don't you?"

"I admit nothing," said Appelsinne stubbornly. "Anyway, it is no crime to want to kill Palook."

"I am not accusing you of any crime," said Quill patiently. "I am only trying to get at the facts. We know," he bluffed, "that when you went up on the balcony you had a revolver with you."

It worked. "You know that?"

"We do."

"Then I deceive you no longer," said Appelsinne graciously. "It is true I went to kill Palook. But you cannot do anything to me for that."

"And what made you change your mind?"

Appelsinne shrugged. "I just change. I think—maybe Pavel come back to me anyway—so I decide to let Palook live."

"It was not," said Quill gently, "because Pavel came and stopped you?"

Appelsinne threw up his arms in despair. "You police, you know everything."

"Almost everything," corrected Quill. "So much, that you cannot help yourself or Pavel by hiding anything now. We are bound to find out anyway and it will be better if you tell us yourself."

Appelsinne hesitated. "You suspect Pavel?"

"We suspect nobody," said Quill. "All we want is facts. If Pavel is guilty your silence will not help. If he is innocent you will only harm him by not speaking."

Appelsinne considered again. "All right," he said, "I tell you everything. But remember that Pavel did not do it."

Gradually the story emerged. It was identical with Quill's theory. Pavel, dancing on the stage, had noticed Appelsinne on the roof. Appelsinne had often told Pavel that he would kill his rival and Pavel, seeing him on the balcony, had guessed his intention. Immediately on his exit, when Petroushka lay dead on the stage, Pavel had dashed round and standing on the balcony had called Appelsinne over. He had taken away the gun and ordered him down. Which was just as well, said Appelsinne, for no sooner was he down than he saw Stroganoff hurrying up. Another moment and he'd have been caught and in the heat of the moment that would have meant the sack. As it was, forty-eight hours later, Stroganoff had cooled down sufficiently to let him off with a fine.

"So you see," he added, "I did not do it. And Pavel did not do it either, for he has to come down quick to take his curtains."

Quill nodded. "We have witnesses that he took his curtains."

"Ah," said Appelsinne relieved.

Quill noted the relief with satisfaction. He did not want Appelsinne to know how gravely Pavel was suspected until the case against him was almost complete. And it was almost complete. He handed Appelsinne both his own and Pavel's subpœnas to the inquest to-morrow and carefully explained their meaning. Appelsinne nodded gravely. He was the first man in the company who did not seem to regard the summons as a privileged invitation to a special form of entertainment.

The matter disposed of, Quill returned to his cross-examination.

"By the way," he said almost casually, "has Pavel still got the revolver?"

"Most certainly."

"May I see it?"

"But why not?" Appelsinne produced a dressing-case, unlocked it and passed over a neat, little silver-plated gun. It was obvious that this had not been fired for some time. It meant nothing of course, one way or another—Pavel might easily have had two revolvers, but Quill pretended to be satisfied.

"Not been fired I notice."

"Naturally," said Appelsinne. "I tell you we did not do it."

"Is this the only revolver your master possesses?"

"That is so," Appelsinne nodded. "He buy bigger revolver the last time we were in London, but it got lost long ago."

This being as satisfactory as anything he was likely to hear, there was no need to prolong the interview. Quill thanked Appelsinne for his information and turned to leave.

"Please," said Appelsinne suddenly. "You do me a favour?"

"Yes?"

"You do not speak to my master of this to-day."

Quill had had no intention of approaching Pavel until, and if the time came for his arrest, but this request was so unexpected that he pretended reluctance.

"I say nothing to him myself," said Appelsinne, "and please you say nothing, too, to-day. You see," he explained, "my master must dance *Petroushka* to-night and the audience will be critical. He must dance his best. And if he knows he has been suspect—it will upset him—he will be excited. And that is bad for dancing. So please you say nothing till after the programme."

This suited Quill's plans beautifully. He pretended to hesitate and then consented. Appelsinne shook him warmly by the hand.

For no reason at all Quill suddenly felt a cad.

CHAPTER X

QUILL lunched alone. The revolver Stanley had found was at Scotland Yard, with one of those experts that can hang you on a scratch, bending double over it. Another sleuth, armed with Pavel's photographs, was visiting the gunsmith's where the revolver had been purchased. Stanley was in his seventh heaven, frightfully busy, checking irrelevant details of quite three-quarters of the company. Arenskaya had been shaken off and Stroganoff had shown no signs of wanting to come. Quill enjoyed his momentary solitude. His mind was almost made up. If the revolver should prove to be the one that killed Palook and its owner identified as Pavel, he would risk its unusual repository and arrest Pavel. After all, an overflowing waste-paper basket was not such a bad hiding place; as a rule the contents would be transferred to the dustbin in one vast heave. Pavel mig: t thus have relied on the revolver getting carried away with the other refuse.

It was not very satisfactory but the rest of the evidence was very strong.

However, he still had to find out why Stroganoff had omitted to tell him that he had seen Pavel on the balcony.

So that afternoon he made his way back to the Collodium and found it in the throes of an audition.

* * * * *

There are two sorts of audition. The more remunerative is presided over by a large cigar, beaming approvingly at every blonde head that bobs beseechingly at it, noting—why, nobody has yet discovered—the names and addresses of hard-working brunettes, refreshing itself distastefully from a large glass of water, and reminding everybody in sight that it has been in the business for twenty years. The other kind of audition is a test of dancing.

The Ballets Stroganoff as usual had its own variant. Arenskaya stood at the side of the stage frightening the girls out of their wits, while Stroganoff sat importantly in the centre chair and promptly turned down anybody of whom Stanley approved. This method, as a rough working rule, was sound enough.

The present audition was held to engage dancers for his winter season at the Casino de la Bazouche. To Stroganoff's continued amazement, few dancers who had survived a season at la Bazouche ever expressed the desire to go through another. Always he had to bribe—some with offers of small parts, others with infinitesimal rises in salary—and still many departed always, and always he had to search for fresh talent. The search was always arduous.

He glared his disgust at a girl from Streatham who was doing her best to register Spanish Passion.

"Your address," he said. "Your name," he added as an afterthought.

He sat engulfed in a sea of gloom, wearily submitting to a Russian Gipsy, a Columbine, a fiendish Tarantella (with not a bell missing from its conscientious tambourine) and even withstood a classical soloist, aloof in pale pink. But at the trickle of certain well-known limpid notes from the piano, he stirred ominously. Soon his worst fears were realized. Came a pair of threshing arms, a wobbling *pas-de-bourrée*, the whole surmounted by a tufted ballet frock.

"*Non!*" groaned Stroganoff. "*Non. Assez de Pavlova. Arretez! Arretez tout de suite!* Go away." He flapped his irate hands at the terrified swan. "Get you out. You shall not even leave your address."

"I go now," he said to Arenskaya. "I have suffered enough. You finish—and send to me the girls that are least bad. I arrange the contracts. Goodbye." He waved an escaping hand and disappeared quickly. Quill followed and caught up with him outside his office.

"Go away," said Stroganoff, not too hopefully. "I am in conference with myself."

"Shan't keep you a moment," said Quill easily and followed him in. Stroganoff with Russian resignation accepted his entry.

"Wiskyansoda," he murmured absently.

"There isn't any," said the experienced Quill.

"No," said Stroganoff. "All right—then we have Russian tea." He pressed a bell. Nothing happened.

"Please don't trouble," Quill assured him. "I don't want any."

"But *moi*—I want it," said Stroganoff. "I want it very much." He put his finger on the bell-push and kept it there for fully half a minute.

"Poof," he said suddenly, "I remember now—it is out of order. *N'importe*—we use the telephone."

Quill waited patiently while he wrestled with the obnoxious instrument.

"I want," he enunciated carefully, "three spoonfuls of the best Souchon. You will add *des citrons* cut *mais très mince*— some sugar—*de l'eau bien bouillante* and . . ."

"Russian tea," said a curt voice. "Oke!"

This weighty matter satisfactorily settled, Stroganoff sank back in his chair and beamed at Quill. He was himself again.

"Good mornings," he said. "You have come to thank me for my *Lac des Cygnes*, no? All right—I listen while you tell me how much you like."

"I'm afraid," said Quill, "I'm here to investigate Palook's death."

"Still?" said Stroganoff, astonished. "Me—I hardly recall it. It is regrettable," he conceded, "but the ballet it must go on."

"You told me yesterday," said Quill, "that you went up on the balcony in the last act."

Stroganoff pondered. "Doubtless you are right," he agreed, "but me I do not remember."

Quill jogged his memory. "You had seen Appelsinne up there."

"Ah, *oui*," said Stroganoff. "I recollect now. I see him. And yesterday I fine him five hundred francs. But alas! I owe him three *mille*, so it do not help me mooch."

"When you reached the balcony, Appelsinne had already left it?"

"He was lucky. Otherwise—maybe I lose the temper and then I am terrible."

"Who was on the balcony when you arrived?"

Any doubts that Quill felt that Stroganoff might not have seen Pavel up there, vanished with the question. It took the impresario fully two seconds to answer and then he said that he did not remember.

"But you remember seeing Appelsinne from the front?"

"*Oui.*"

"And you remember going up on the balcony?"

"*Certainement.*"

"And Appelsinne was not there?"

"*Non.*"

"But who was there?"

"Me," said Stroganoff cleverly.

"And who else?"

There was a knock at the door.

"Ah," said Stroganoff, "the tea."

But it was Stanley. For the first time in this record Stroganoff was pleased to see him.

"Ah," he beamed, "I give you now to Stanley. Stanley he very clever boy. He show you everything. Good-bye."

Quill could deal with that easily. He winked at Stanley.

"Go away," he said. And Stanley, delighted, made stealthily for the door.

"Now," he turned back to his task grimly, "will you tell me who you saw on the balcony?"

"*Mais, personne.*"

"Then I will tell you."

Stroganoff crumpled—but only slightly.

"If you know," he said defiantly, "why you ask?"

There was a knock at the door.

"Ah," said Stroganoff, "the tea."

But it was Puthyk, come to complain that Pavel was dancing Petroushka that night.

"When I dance Petroushka so magnificent yesterday," he explained, "I say to myself—I am superb. Surely our wise director, Stroganoff, will now see that I must dance the part. But you are still blind. You have give him to Pavel, who dance even worse than Anton."

To Quill's surprise Stroganoff did not seem annoyed. With extraordinary gentleness he put an arm round the old man's shoulders, led him to the door, and pushed him out in Russian.

"That one—he was a great dancer, a great artist," he began hopefully. "If you like I tell you his history."

But even as Quill tried to prevent the launching, the door opened again.

The new arrival was well built but not well dressed. He

had magnificent shoulders and a yellow polo sweater, the physique of a Greek god and old flannel trousers, the pale cast of thought of a Gielgud, with the beaming spiritual spectacles of a J. B. Priestley, a shock of black hair and one sock coming down. He was already talking.

"I have been inspired with the most colossal idea that ever happened to anybody," he announced to the unintroduced Quill.

"Come in and propound it," said Stroganoff gratefully. "Sit down. Have a cigarette. You are not in a hurry—no?"

The intellectual relaxing, slightly dazed, into an arm-chair, remarked that he was in no hurry at all.

"I present you," burbled Stroganoff, "to M'sieu Quill. He is a great lover of the ballet and also a policeman. For you M'sieu Quill," he said in ringing tones, "you have the pleasure to meet the choreographer of the future—Nicholas Nevajno— whose work you must learn to love though—alas! it take time and much money. We will now listen to his new idea."

"It is superb," said the choreographer of the future, modestly. "I tell you. But first you schange me small scheque?"

"No," said Stroganoff.

"Olright," said Nevajno, not noticeably disappointed, "I still tell you. This morning I find a paper in the bus so I read it. It was a long journey," he explained apologetically, "and I had no book. And I notice that the red shirts they are angry—and the black shirts they are angry too. The brown shirts they are making speeches, the yellow shirts, they are insulted, and the green shirts, they may not wear it. All the nations, all the politics, all the armies—it is shirts. Very well, I decide, we will make the symbolic ballet with many shirts."

"How many shirts?" asked Stroganoff apprehensively.

"Not many," said Nevajno. "Say—four dozen."

"Two dozen," bartered Stroganoff. "Silk—it is expensive."

"These, they will not be in silk," said Nevajno grandly.

"Silk is not modern. They shall be of aluminium. That is settled. The first scene," he went on, "it is New York in a hundred years. The skyscrapers, they are twice as high. We have one on the back-cloth. The setting it is constructivist. Upstairs a big aeroplane with machine gun. Downstairs a prison. That, too, is symbolic. Then we see the Dictator in orange shirt."

"Pavel," said Stroganoff.

"It is possible. He dance an oration to the *corps de ballet*, who wear the bandages round the mouth. That, too, is symbolic. The next scene . . ."

"Another scene," said Stroganoff. "You ruin me!"

"*Mais oui*," Nevajno was not at all put out. "There will be seven scenes and an apotheosis. Each shall have its shirt and a back-cloth that is unique."

Stroganoff groaned.

"All the best composers they shall write the score. Stravinsky, Ravel, Prokofiev, Honegger, Poulenc and maybe Constant Lambert. Picasso shall do the *décor* and Peter Arno the *rideau*. Never will the world see a ballet like it."

"Never shall they see it," agreed Stroganoff, recovering his senses.

"But it is colossal."

"It ruin me."

There was a pause.

"Olright," said Nevajno. He did not seem unduly downcast by the repudiation of his child. Almost one might have said he had expected it. "In that case, I ask you a favour. Now that you save the expense of production—you schange me small scheque till Wednesday?"

"No."

"Olright," said Nevajno philosophically. He turned to Quill. "Per'aps you schange it?"

"No," said Quill.

"Olright," said Nevajno—and went.

"That one," said the ever-hopeful Stroganoff, "is a great artist, too. If you like I tell you his story."

But Quill had had quite enough of this.

"On the contrary," he said, "you will tell me that you saw Pavel on the balcony."

Stroganoff leapt to his histrionic feet. "The scoundrel— he was there? Then I fine him too. I cannot think," he added, "how I come to overlook him."

"Neither can I," said Quill, "particularly as he was in the Moor's make-up."

"The balcony it was dark."

"On the contrary, it was well lit."

"I did not have my glasses."

"I have never seen you use them yet."

"I was looking at the conductor."

"Have a heart," said Quill. "There is no point in keeping this up. You will save us both time if you admit that you saw Pavel on the balcony. You are not even helping Pavel by lying. I have several witnesses who saw him up there."

Stroganoff abandoned his amateur theatricals and looked annoyed.

"Inspective Detector," he snapped, "you should have tell me this before. Then I not try to lead you round the gooseberry bush."

"It was not a very wise thing to attempt anyway," said Quill. Somehow he could never get cross with this man. "Why did you try it?"

"But it is simple," said Stroganoff. "If I tell you that I see Pavel on the balcony with a gun, you think that Pavel shoot Anton and then, maybe, you arrest him—no? And who then shall dance *Petroushka* on Wednesday week before Benois himself—if he come? You say, poof! that is not important. You are the policeman. All you desire is someone to hang. But me, I am an artist and business man. And if Pavel cannot dance there is none to take his place."

"But if Pavel murdered Palook?"

"What does it matter to me who killed Anton?" asked Stroganoff not unreasonably. "He is dead and we must find other dancer for *Petroushka*. And that is Pavel. So we cannot afford that the police they interfere. I tell Saussisson that I see Pavel on balcony," he confided, "and he tell me to guard my hair. So I decide I tell nothing till Wednesday week. After that, I say, I hide nothing no longer. Even though it mean I have to find new dancer, I tell police everything."

Expressed like that, Quill felt that this was really rather handsome of him.

"But," said Stroganoff, "you find out and everything is lost. Please," he looked at Quill appealingly, "you do me favour—no? You do not arrest Pavel till after Wednesday week?"

"It is not yet certain that we shall arrest him at all," said Quill, "and if you are wise you will not mention the matter to Pavel. It might," he added cunningly, "upset his dancing."

To this Stroganoff nodded judiciously.

"You are right, *mon cher*," he agreed. "He is not as calm as I."

*　　*　　*　　*　　*

At the Yard, Quill was informed that his chief wanted to see him. Quill was not amused. His chief, he thought, ought to have been a ballet critic, for he had now reached the enviable position from which he had nothing to do but criticize the efforts of others. This duty he performed with the detachment of a Constant Lambert and the invective of a James Agate—though unfortunately not in French. Still, thought Quill, even his chief could not grumble at an arrest within forty-eight hours. That is, if he could make the arrest.

He interviewed the gun expert who produced a series of photographic plates, all of them identical to the casual eye, which, he assured Quill, proved conclusively that the revolver Stanley had found was the one that killed Palook. So far so good.

Better still, the sleuth who had been to the gunsmith returned with the news that the gunsmith—an awfully decent fellow who had only missed the sleuth at Marlborough by some fifteen years—had picked out Pavel immediately from the bunch of photographs handed to him. His books recorded that the revolver had been sold two years ago, the exact date being August 17, 1935. He recalled the transaction distinctly as the purchasers were not the sort of clients who generally came to his shop—or indeed, ever. Pavel had been accompanied by an amiable bald-headed gentleman who said "Poof" and would try to test the gun before they reached the shooting gallery. The latter had also been fascinated by an old cannon which he had tried his hardest to persuade the gunsmith to fire, promising to buy it—by instalments—if he liked the noise.

Fortified with this information, which he felt clinched the case, Quill entered the chief's sanctum hopefully.

"Sit down," said a cold voice behind the desk. It did not say "wiskyansoda." It did not enquire "you have slept well —no?" But at least it did not expect him to drink Russian tea.

"I've been reading over your scanty reports," said the Snarl, "and it seems to me that it ought to be a fairly simple case. And I almost envy you working amid that fascinating background. It reminds me," said the Snarl, suddenly human, "of the St. Petersburg pearls case, when I took the divine Arenskaya out to supper."

"Who?" said Quill, startled.

"It was before your time," said the Snarl condescendingly. "She was a famous dancer and, very, very beautiful. Mind you, she had a will of her own."

"She still has," said Quill.

"So beautiful," went on the Snarl, oblivious, "that I could

not find it in my heart to be cross with her when the stolen pearls turned out to be a stunt for the papers—the first of its kind, I believe. Ah, she was beautiful, beautiful," he sighed. "And what is more, she like me."

"She likes me too," said Quill. "But alas, she is no longer so beautiful. She's with the Stroganoff company now," he explained.

The Snarl was suddenly interested. It had half a mind to run down to the theatre and renew old acquaintances.

"They are giving *Petroushka* to-night," said Quill. "You have seen *Petroushka*—no?"

The Snarl looked startled. It was not customary for its subordinates to use such curious English.

"Not for ages," it admitted boyishly. "Book me two seats for to-night. No—one seat," it amended.

Quill, who by this time had lost all sense of caution, asked if he should ring up a florist as well. But this, though clearly a good idea, savoured too much of levity to please the Snarl. It scribbled a hasty memo and returned to its official displeasure.

"What have you to report—if anything?"

"Sir," said Quill, "I would like to apply for a warrant for the arrest of Pavel Bunia of the Stroganoff company. . . ."

*   *   *   *   *

"*Mais, mon cher,*" said Stroganoff for the fifteenth time. "*Soyez raisonable.* There is no one else to dance Petroushka."

"Very sorry," said Quill for the sixteenth time.

Stroganoff was in despair. He paced the office like a fog-bound captain on an uninsured deck, waving his arms and letting his Russian tea get cold on the table. You felt that if he'd had any hair, he'd have been tearing it.

"But you promise me that you do not make the arrest till after Wednesday week!"

"Sorry," said Quill.

"And now you will not even wait till after the performance to-night."

"Sorry," said Quill.

"The tickets they are sold, the dancers they are ready, the audience it comes dam' quick and—poof—there is no *Petroushka*."

"Sorry."

"I have to return all the moneys and again I am broke. You do not wish that—no?"

"Sorry," said Quill inexorably.

"But," said Stroganoff, trying a different tack, "what for you is the difference? You wish to arrest Pavel now—I consent that you arrest him at *minuit moins quart*, so now we are agreed. Let us," he suggested, "forget our quarrel. Wiskyansoda?"

"There isn't any," said Quill.

"*Mais, si*," said Stroganoff, opening and shutting drawers with an air of an absent-minded conjurer who has forgotten where he put the vanished lady. "*Voilà!*" Proudly he deposited a bottle on the table.

"Say why?" he said, squirting the soda experimentally.

"I'm sorry," said Quill, "but your request is impossible. It is entirely without precedent to postpone an arrest for the sake of a performance."

"It is entirely without precedent," retorted Stroganoff with dignity, "to take away a Petroushka before he even start."

"Sorry."

"You refuse."

"I refuse."

"You are frighten that he escape. But that," said Stroganoff, "is stupid. *Imbécile*. He is on stage all the time—he will not go till he take his curtains and when he come off—poof— you catch him. That is agreed then? But," and fresh despair overcame him, "who shall dance *Petroushka* on Wednesday week, I really cannot think."

Quill began to feel sorry for the old boy. After all, he reasoned, what did it really matter if he postponed the arrest. And he was certainly likely to get Pavel away with less fuss and trouble if he waited till after the performance.

"All right," he said, "I agree. After the performance."

In his relief Stroganoff drank the whisky and soda.

CHAPTER XI

As usual, that uncanny psychologist Hiram B. Sausage, had been right. The Great British Public did not, as Stanley prophesied, refuse to stand for a second performance of *Petroushka* so close on the heels of the tragedy. Indeed, they stood for hours, in talkative serried ranks. By eight-fifteen the house was almost packed. There was a curdling of mothers, a hesitancy of fathers, an edging away of critics, all society, all the intelligentsia—but we dealt with this in the opening chapter. The only notable addition this evening was Quill's chief, the Snarl, miraculously transformed into a blush behind a bunch of orchids.

"Ah," shrilled a voice, as he puffed his way laboriously across the foyer, "it is my ol' friend Jellybags."

It was Arenskaya, resplendent in a Spanish shawl (*Good Humoured Ladies*), a Russian tiara (*Oiseau de Feu*), and an ostrich egg pearl necklace (*Scheherazade*), and a red silk evening dress (her own). The Snarl blushed deeper and, old Continental memories stirring, bent gallantly to kiss her hand. It only just managed it.

"You 'ave got fat," said Arenskaya frankly.

"You, Madame, are more fascinating than ever," announced the Snarl, getting into its stride and presenting the orchids with a portly flourish. Arenskaya pounced on them with shrill cries of ecstasy.

Her pleasure gratified the blush. It was not so gratified, however, to observe Quill standing a few yards away and looking every bit as pleased. It became definitely annoyed when Arenskaya beckoned Quill over, and it was the last straw when she introduced them.

"This," she said proudly, "is M'sieur Jellybags. His other name I forget."

"I know it," said Quill.

"He and I were very great friends," began Arenskaya with unusual delicacy. "But that long time ago. I do not think he so good in bed now," she finished, making up for it.

"Not at all," declared the blush, too confused to know exactly what it was it wanted to deny.

Quill could not remember when he had last enjoyed himself so much. Gallantly he resisted the temptation of digging his chief in the ribs and calling him a gay old dog.

"Well, well," he said jovially, "I must not intrude on this providential reunion," and he bolted, blissfully unaware that by so doing, he missed overhearing what must surely have been the most unusual invitation ever handed out to an elderly Scotland Yard official.

"Next autumn," said Arenskaya, "I am forty-one."

At this outrageous statement the blush was almost transformed back to the Official Snarl with a passion for facts and an uncomfortable memory for figures, but it stopped itself just in time.

"Impossible," it said ambiguously.

"*Pas de blague*," said Arenskaya delighted. "It is true. And to celebrate it I give a little dinner in Vienna. *Trente deux couverts*. The only woman there, it is me, and the only men it is my lovers. My 'usband he preside. You make me the compliment of coming? You are the favourite of all my lovers." She took his acceptance for granted and linked her arm fondly through his. "And now you come with me to my box and you will see that no ballerina to-day can dance like I dance once."

The Snarl came quietly.

*   *   *   *   *

Already the house lights were fading. The curtains, thick folded shadows, veiled the stage. Soon the opening chords of a Chopin Prelude filled the theatre with a sweet sad nostalgia.

"'Ush," said Arenskaya unnecessarily. The Snarl looked hurt.

The shadows parted gently to reveal a group of Sylphs in a moonlit glade. Wearing the long white ballet skirts of a Taglioni, her small brittle wings, stood Rubinska, her *corps de ballet* grouped lovingly around her, and to the sound of the Nocturne the old print stirred to life.

Les Sylphides is a ballet of mood rather than of movement. It is the visible animation of a sigh. Its dances are the coveted prizes of the company. By her *Sylphides* shall ye know her, can be said of the Ballerina.

The lovely line of the *arabesque*, the aerial flight of the *jeté*, the perpetual surprise of the *developpé*—lightness, neatness, and a sense of abstract role, all are called for in *Les Sylphides*.

With the first bars of the Nocturne, the group dissolves into two lines. Now the first line is moving deftly forward on the point. Now they kneel. Now the second line advances on the point between the kneeling figures. Now they crystallize into groups once more.

Soon Kasha will be dancing with his two ballerinas, Rubinska, dark and brilliant, and Lubova, with a divine *developpé*, and the determined air of an Elizabeth Bergner sharing a close-up with a Marlene Dietrich.

"Lovely, lovely," sighed the Snarl.

"In *Les Sylphides*," said Arenskaya, "all that matters is the make-up—*mais Giselle, c'est autre chose*. I remember when I dance 'er at the Maryinsky. . . ."

But the Snarl's eyes were on the stage where the Girl with the Impeccable Technique and the Implacable Mother was studiously putting over the first valse.

And since this seems as good a moment as any, let us look at her by no means unique career.

The Girl with the Impeccable Technique is first to be seen, aged about five, an anxious expression surmounting an unsteady pose in the window of the local photographer. By the time she is ten she will have won every competition in sight.

So far nothing has been called for from The Implacable Mother, save possibly an enigmatic expression, and the modest disclaimer, "Anna always wins." This basilisk gaze is, however, merely the portent of the calm before the storm. Some pretty strenuous years lie ahead of Momma.

Soon Anna finds herself being ferried from one expostulating management to the other, leaving a trail of broken contracts in her wake. She is levered from the *corps de ballet*, trailed through *demi-caractère*, and hoisted into a species of *Matinée* performance Ballerinadom. She has been with Stroganoff for seven weeks, and already Momma is getting a little restive.

And so by this time is the audience, for, though her background is the tranced *corps de ballet*, and though her dancing is meticulously neat, her points twin rocks that no amount of blundering breakers can displace, her arms now taut, now curving, but always with an academic correctitude, her *relevés* relentlessly on the beat, somehow her performance seems uninspired.

"To-morrow, I give 'er 'ell," observed Arenskaya with relish, "and 'er Mother she take 'er off to Buttonhooke."

Now the *corps de ballet* frames the stage, as Rubinska comes flying on in the first Mazurka. The long white ballet skirts and the tiny wings, and her manner of turning her sleek little head as she rises from the stage, turn the proscenium arch once more into the frame for a print of Taglioni. She rises on wings, and her points cut the air. Or she travels across the stage on the tapering pink satin ballet shoe, and all is poetry.

It was almost a pity that the Snarl had no moustachio. Undoubtedly he would have twirled it here.

Kasha Ranevsky was dancing the man in *Sylphides* to-night. He invested the simple role with a sense of style that argued well for his future. In a fair wig and the black coat and flowing white sleeves of the Benois design, he took the stage like a veteran. The knowing in the audience turned approvingly to one another.

Arenskaya said: "'is coat it is too tight," and left it at that.

Now Rubinska returns to dance the *pas-de-deux* valse with him. She floats in his arms on to the stage, a white petal, tossed upon a summer's breeze. Presently she will fly from him, a white moth taken by the candle-flame of the footlights, and he will gently, caressingly, draw her back to safety by her two tiny wings.

Together they depart, and Shura Lubova enters to dance the prelude. Shura was a young St. Joan, her questing dictated by her "voices." She danced as one dedicated to some compelling purpose. The tenderness, the lightness, and the disarming eagerness, that is so implicit in the accepted reading of the wistful little role, was missing from this performance. Shura's was the expression of a single-minded saint—the passage of a fanatic.

"She is pale to-night, Shurushka," Arenskaya observed. "I t'ink it is for love of Pavel—what a pity—she is a girl of good sense—plenty courage—but with 'im she be'ave like a little virgin."

And now the mood that Shura had created was dissipated by the entrance of the sylphs in the moonlit finale. The curtain descended upon a tableau of frozen loveliness. Rubinska with her head on Kasha's shoulder. Shura beside him,[1] and around her, grouped lovingly, the immobility of the *corps de ballet*.

The slow swish of the descending curtain summed up the ballet with its whispered sigh.

*   *   *   *   *

Up in the star's dressing-room Pavel was giving a display of that temperament that had endeared him to so many of his enemies. He cursed the solicitous Appelsinne, he cursed his wig-maker, he cursed the London weather, and, just for luck, he cursed Stroganoff. Here he was, in his first really important role in London, and he had had to pay for his own wreath.

"When you have had the success," Appelsinne assured him, "we ask for more salary."

"And we not get," said Pavel, struggling furiously into his clown's costume. "Already that *succinsin*[2] owes me a fortune."

The *succinsin* bustled in just in time to overhear the last sentence.

"Who owe you money?" he enquired indignantly. "You tell me and I stop it from their salary. Unless, of course," he amended hastily, "you have schanged scheque for Nevajno. There I can do nothing. Already he owe me moneys."

Nervous as he was Pavel still found time to wonder how Nevajno had achieved this miracle. Eventually he enquired. But Stroganoff, who had been caught once, was giving away no secrets.

"I go now," he said, and stumbled over Shura Lubova, who, fresh from her triumph in *Sylphides*, was entering in a dressing-gown. He wagged a roguish finger at her.

"Not before the performance," he said.

[1] In the Ballets Stroganoff it is the custom for the Prelude Ballerina to pair with the Ballerina of the *Pas-de-deux*. The Ballerina of the Valse reclines impartially at their feet.

[2] Russian expression implying illegitimate birth.

"I will see to that," said Appelsinne grimly, transfixing Shura with a look that would have scared anybody except a ballet dancer out of the room at once.

But Shura was long inured to a certain amount of unpopularity from Pavel's friends. She advanced unwaveringly.

"You look magnificent," she said to Pavel, who, owing to the heavy clown's make-up, did, as a matter of fact, look slightly less revolting than usual. "It should be I who dance the doll with you to-night."

"That was impossible," said Pavel curtly.

"Did you ask Stroganoff as you promise me?"

"Pavel promise you nothing," broke in Appelsinne roughly. "And anyhow Stroganoff would laugh at the idea. And me I laugh too—ha! ha! As a dancer you do not compare with Rubinska."

Shura's lips tightened. "Do you think so too?" she asked Pavel.

Pavel hesitated. He looked helplessly from Appelsinne to Shura and from Shura to Appelsinne.

"Yes," he said, weakly.

"You skunk," said Shura, "you low, crawling, abject worm. You are frightened of your dresser. You are terrified to go near a woman because of him. You've been terrified ever since Anton was shot—and what's more I shouldn't be surprised if you knew who shot him and why."

"Me, I suppose," said Appelsinne. "I laugh. Ha! Ha!"

"Yes—you."

"You shall not insult my Serge," said Pavel, whitely.

"Oh, you needn't worry," said Shura. "I shan't tell the police. I do not need the police to look after me."

"You go away," said Appelsinne. "You are upsetting my master."

"I will upset him a lot more before I've done."

"Another threat," said Appelsinne, "always she threaten and always I laugh. Ha-ha! And she never do nothing."

"Never," agreed Shura more gently, "until one day you'll drive me just a little too far and that day," she eyed Pavel, "I'll kill you."

The call boy put an end to the irregular triangle. With a whisk of her dressing-gown Shura vanished. Pavel applied the finishing touches to his face and made his way down to the stage. The curtain would be up in a few minutes. Rubinska was already in her booth and Nevajno, who had secured the role of the Moor, was entering his. Pavel scowled at them both impartially, entered his booth, and settled into his arm rest to await his cue.

Judge then of the crack in his perilous calm caused by the strong smell of brilliantine and Volti-Subito. The conductor's face smiled evilly at him round the canvas edges of the puppet booth.

"Hello, big boy," said Volti, every inch the villain. "So this is your great chance—eh? Only not while I'm conducting."

* * * * *

A new Petroushka will always draw your connoisseur, though judging from their noncommittal attitude, the connoisseurs to-night were not expecting too much. The balleto-medico, in fact, went so far as to declare that he had only turned up for the sake of his collection. He collected dancers as other men collected stamps; all the choicer specimens of Petroushka were already affixed in his album and he only needed Pavel for a swop. The rest of the audience seemed to be in much the same frame of mind and, as the orchestra broke into the opening bars, even Stroganoff sensed that this evening, though financially a good thing, was unlikely to prove an artistic success.

"My orchestra it play well—no?" he said, but without much conviction. And was plunged deeper into gloom when Stanley agreed with him.

D

"Go away," he said, and, as Stanley lingered: "Bring me a list."

"What list, sir?"

"Any list," said Stroganoff, turning wearily back to the stage where maids, moujiks, women, children, coachmen, nurses, merchants and gipsies were drifting conscientiously about the booth-ringed square. The audience seemed but vaguely aware of them. So, too, but less pardonably, did the conductor.

"That one—I sack him," muttered Stroganoff as Volti-Subito passed a hand over his hair, straightened his tie, and flicked a wrist vaguely in the direction of the big drum, who had already entered two beats ago and was audibly trying to make up his mind whether to start all over again or ignore the episode entirely.

"This is like old times," said the Snarl fondly to the stupefied Arenskaya. He was not particularly musical.

On the stage the organ grinder churned out his tune. The street dancers went slickly through their routine. From the balcony, the gipsies threw coins at them. In the wings, Sergeant Banner felt uneasily in his pockets.

From behind the curtains, steps the magician. He pipes a wily tune on a reed, the flautist, oblivious, two bars behind him. The curtains part and—lo!—the puppets loll inanimate in their cells. Rubinska—eager in her stillness. The Moor —Nevajno—obviously thinking of something else. And Petroushka, his face so quiet it might have been a mask.

"Pip-pip" goes the flute, and the Moor, abandoning the problem he is working on, springs jerkily into life.

"Pip-pip" Rubinska is on her points.

"Pip-pip" but Petroushka still lolls inanimate.

"What did I tell you?" said the balleto-medico with satisfaction, "he's missed his cue."

"Pip-pip" went the flute again a trifle impatiently.

But Petroushka took no notice of his master. He was

huddled in his cell. A dark stain was beginning to appear on the side of his white clown's tunic.

The magician took a step forward, touched him gingerly, and withdrew gazing fascinated at a hand that was red and wet.

The crowd swept forward.

"Curtain," screamed Arenskaya from her box.

*   *   *   *   *

Pavel was dead. He had been shot through the back in line with his heart. Death, whenever it had been administered, must have been instantaneous.

Quill looked at the body. The company, silent, stood about in small groups. The Snarl came hurrying over, behind him Arenskaya and Stroganoff. Speechlessly they ranged themselves beside Quill.

It was Stroganoff who broke the silence.

"What a pity," he said. "Just as you were going to arrest him, too."

CHAPTER XII

THOUGH Palook went to his grave with a grouch at the scant notice taken by the world of his quitting it, Pavel had no such grievance. His was definitely a front page story. The murder of two dancers—in the same ballet, in the same role, at the same theatre, within four days of each other, roused the Press to a height of enthusiasm that had never been reached by their performances in it. The regular ballet critics were gently brushed aside and Ace Crime reporters rushed out to take their places. They did their job well. From the masterly scare lines (A Bullet in the Ballet. Another Clown Dances to Death.) through pulsating paragraphs (. . . still, lifeless, with a slow red patch seeping through his blouse, the clown lay dead. . . . Pavel Bunia would dance no more. . . .), past the stricken comments of the company ("I loved him," says Arenskaya),[1] to a highly imaginative picture of a vengeful Stroganoff vowing to give up vodka till he had laid the murderer by his *entrechats*. . . . It was a lovely story. If Pavel had any complaint it could only have been that his dancing abilities were not noticeably stressed.

Even the Fleet Street News Editors seemed satisfied and one of them, happily relegating Liberia's appeal to the League of Nations to the gossip columns, was actually overheard to remark that it made good reading. Dazed by their success, the reporters staggered out to consolidate their position. They interviewed Hiram B. Sausage, who with a fine impartiality distributed photos, not only of Pavel but of the rest of the company. They interviewed Appelsinne, who refused to talk. They interviewed Puthyk, who refused to stop. They interviewed Rubinska, Shura, and the Implacable Mother. They interviewed Stanley and got tired first. They chased Stroganoff all over the theatre till he sought refuge in the orchestra pit, only to give himself away by picking out "Otchi Tchernia" with one finger on the piano. They made whoopee with Sergeant Banner, and mocked at Quill's guarded statements. And then, their appetites still unappeased, they all turned up at the inquest on Anton Palook.

The Coroner, Mr. A. Zzugg, whose only distinction up to date was that his was the last name in the telephone book, welcomed them with gusto. This time, he felt, he had definitely put one over on a certain colleague. Had that colleague, he thought, but foreseen the second murder, doubtless he would have wangled Palook's corpse into his own district —if necessary with his own hands. But he had carelessly failed to anticipate it and now he, Zzugg, had the opportunity to get some of his own observations on the front page.

[1] Actually she said: "I loathed him," but a tactful sub-editor altered this.

The court was packed. Fifty happy reporters and a complacent coroner did much to dissipate the formal atmosphere
that is so much in evidence on those occasions. While it
could not be called a fashionable inquest—"eccentric" describes
it admirably. The front seats in the spectators' sections had
been pinched by a whiskered froth of Russian generals, the
mothers, well to the fore from force of habit, were just
behind them, while the company, the orchestra and those
balletomanes who were not already queueing up outside the
Collodium, took up the remaining seats. Poor Mr. Jones[1] of
Muswell Hill, who never missed an inquest, found himself,
to his annoyance, pushed against a wall next to a young man
sporting a perfume that even his wife would not dream of
using.

In the well of the court an ostrich feather waved magnificently.

"It is 'ot," said Arenskaya, and Puthyk, taking over the
fan, waved eloquently.

"This reminds me," he said, "of Salome."

It was a fascinating theme. "When I dance 'er in Monte
Carlo," began Arenskaya to Stroganoff.

But Stroganoff was oblivious. He had many other things
to think about. His finances seemed to be improving. The
house would be packed to-night and the night after. But
who would dance *Petroushka* on Wednesday week to Benois
himself, if he come? He had not had time to have his lemon
tea this morning. And why would they not wait for him to
put on his admiral's uniform before they take his photo
yesterday? How they lie these papers. They called Stanley
his right-hand man.

"It is not true," his anguish burst out.

"*Mais si c'est vrai*," corrected Arenskaya, "when I was
at the sixth veil the Prince he could stand the suspense no
longer."

"Poof!" said Stroganoff, and went back to his broodings.

* Not the one you know.

Ernest Smithsky would now demand to dance *Petroushka*. Beads of horror broke out at the presentiment.

Nevajno was looking round the court hopefully. These people who had been so obliging yesterday, here they all were. He must talk to them gain. Happily he fingered his diminished cheque book.

A frantic usher was telling Quill that he had been quite unable to keep the witnesses out of the courtroom. In spite of his protests they had swept magnificently past him, announcing that the management had presented them with complimentary seats.[1] Quill gave Banner his instructions and watched grimly while he dealt with the expostulating Stroganoff, Kasha and the affable Puthyk. He was too fed up to extract any amusement from the Sergeant's battle.

He felt heavily responsible for Pavel's death. If he had not yielded to Stroganoff's blandishments, Pavel would still have been alive. On the other hand it looked now as though he would once again have been arresting the wrong man, and yet the evidence against Pavel had been convincing enough. The revolver, the motive and the time lag—all fitted in. Even his murder could not absolve him entirely of suspicion, but it certainly shook Quill's faith in his guilt.

Last night had not been pleasant. The Snarl had been far from sympathetic. Keeping the company in the theatre till the early hours of the morning had not been easy. The routine interrogations had been laborious and almost profitless. This was one of those ridiculously simple murders that it was impossible to get down to. Somebody—one of the many people that had passed behind the booth—had parked a gun against it, shot Pavel, and left the gun beside it. The gun had been promptly identified by Stanley as his own— he had missed it yesterday but had gleefully decided not to present the police with his own clues—Blast him! No mystery at all as to how the murder was done—only who did it.

[1] "They do this for me because I too am impresario," Stroganoff.

Almost, felt Quill, he would have preferred one of those cases where all the doors and windows were locked and nobody had been near the house; one of those cases where you had only to discover how it was done and the murderer fell into your handcuffs automatically.

Once again his note-book was bristling with names but the Detective's Handbook (Eliminate your suspects with caution) was singularly unhelpful. Quite frankly he had not the remotest idea who had killed either of them. Perhaps when he had had a few quiet hours to think, some theory might present itself. In the meantime he would not stress his suspicions of Pavel to the coroner.

The jury were looking intelligent. In the witness-box the balleto-medico was telling his story. He showed a slight tendency to dwell on artistic details and the coroner, in blissful ignorance of what was coming to him later, was under the impression that he was faced with a difficult witness and was handling him extremely well. He was shocked to learn that the body had been moved at Stroganoff's orders before the police arrived, and made up his mind to deal faithfully with that witness when he came up. He plied the balleto-medico with questions. How did he come to be summoned to the corpse? No public appeal for a doctor had been made to the audience.

"I was called by Mr. Stroganoff's secretary."

"How did he know you were present?"

"Everybody knew," said the balleto-medico with pride. "I am always present at a ballet *première*. I have been present at every ballet *première*—bar one—for the past fifteen years."

"Which one?" asked the coroner, interested in spite of himself.

"Gare du Nord."

"And why was that?"

Nevajno, too, was on his feet hotly demanding an explanation. It was his ballet.

"I was down with 'flu."

"Olright," Nevajno, obviously relieved, subsided into his seat. "For just a moment I fear it was because you do not admire my work."

"I don't," said the balleto-medico.

Nevajno leapt to his feet again.

Order was restored with difficulty.

The police-surgeon who followed struck a more formal note. His evidence was a model of what evidence should be. Cold, curt and precise—nobody listened to it. Following him, Quill confined his evidence to an outline of fact and refused to allow the coroner to lure him into theorizing of any kind. A dull witness, thought the disappointed coroner.

He brightened slightly as Stroganoff took the stand. This one looked much more promising.

"You are," he said, speaking very distinctly as one must when speaking to someone who probably does not understand English very well, "Vladimir Alexander Stroganoff?"

"But of course," said Stroganoff surprised.

"You are the proprietor of the Stroganoff Ballet at present performing at the Collodium theatre?"

"We try to get Covent Garden," explained Stroganoff, a little shamefaced, "but de Basil he get there first. His not bad ballet," he conceded magnanimously, "maybe some day we go into partnership."

"On the night of the sixth," said the coroner firmly, "you gave a performance of a ballet called *Petroushka*. In this ballet Anton Palook was found shot."

"This I know already," said Stroganoff, wearily.

"I understand that it was at your orders that the body was moved from the stage before the police arrived?"

"Of course," beamed Stroganoff, "I give all the orders in my company."

"*Quelle blague*," said Arenskaya loudly.

"Silence," said the usher.

"What made you do this thing?"

Stroganoff looked perplexed. "But what else can I do? Would you wish that I leave poor Anton in the middle of the Ajax *décor*—a ballet that he could never support?"

"He had no taste," shouted Nevajno defiantly, "it is well known."

"Silence," said the usher.

"But were you not aware," pursued the coroner, still sweetly reasonable, "that the police would wish to find everything undisturbed?"

"But the audience very disturbed if they find dead body on stage in my theatre," retorted Stroganoff, "the police, they do not pay for seats. The audience they do—some of them, *au moins*."

"But was it essential to continue the performance that night? With your dancer shot?"

"We do not continue the performance yesterday after Pavel die," said Stroganoff, "and look what happen? Many people they try to get their moneys back. That they fail is caused only by our admirable Mr. Saintly. Ah! *Bonjour, mon ami*," he waved a cordial hand in the direction of a blushing pincenez.

"So," said the coroner less affably, "your box office meant more to you than the death of your leading dancer. You did not care that your action might be helping a murderer to escape."

"The ballet it must go on," said Arenskaya.

"Silence," said the usher.

"*Mais, mon cher*, I put it to you as one artist to another," burbled Stroganoff, "where would my ballet be, if for every little accident we make a stop? We must continue always. In Bled there are riots—but my company it perform every night. Some town in Mexico they kill the president in the *entr'acte* but the Ballet Stroganoff it ignore, and we give the last act to new president. They shoot him too next week —it was sad. In Salonika the orchestra they strike—but we buy good gramophone. And then there was Paris—big night —fashionable audience—all seats paid for—Pilaff was with us then—he dance Petroushka—it was in the bill that night. And then, half-hour before the performance, I go to his dressing-room—and—poof—he is suicided. But do I lose my head? No. We give instead that old favourite *Casse Noisette*—in its entirety. A little under-rehearsed perhaps, but the audience they are pleased. And later I give the role of Petroushka to Anton." He stopped suddenly. "*Tiens!*" he said, "that is curious. My three Petroushkas—they are all dead!"

During the scuffle at the Press table that followed, Quill passed a note to the coroner. The coroner nodded.

"This Mr.—er—Pilaff," he asked, "you say he committed suicide? What form of suicide?"

"He shoot himself."

"What was his reason for suicide?"

"Who can tell why an artist kill himself?" asked Stroganoff. "May be he love someone who do not love him. We all very excited about it at time—but it is soon over and we go back to work. Our work," said Stroganoff, "it is to us everything. We eat, we drink, we love, we kill—but first of all we dance. A dancer," he went on, warming to his theme. . . .

Quill began to feel a certain sympathy for the coroner. He had been through it himself.

Stroganoff was now well in his stride. Words cascaded from him in a mingled stream of French, Russian, and occasionally, English. The coroner bleated at him pathetically, the clerk rallied to him with a series of shocked "hushes," but they might as well have tried to stop a sports car at an amber light.

They were sympathetic, these English. They listened. Clearly they were impressed by his theory that *Pagliacci* would have been more convincing as a ballet. . . .

It was a naturalized juryman who rescued the court. He shouted something in Russian. The uncouth adjective jerked

Stroganoff out of his stride, he abandoned his discourse and began to reply in kind. Both subsided. The coroner, taking no further chances, dismissed the witness hurriedly. This was not the curtain Stroganoff had expected, but after waiting hopefully for a round of applause which did not materialize, he allowed himself to be led away.

But his evidence, extricated from its froth, was the stone that started a great many rings of activity.

Three dead Petroushkas were a lovely gift to the Press. They linked the two London murders, sensational enough in themselves, to the eerie chain of the supernatural—the theme that always fascinates—paving the way to superstition and panic. Already members of the company in court were whispering to each other, speculating, with delightful shivers, upon who would be offered the role next. For Quill the news meant a new factor in his enquiry, the despatch of telegrams to Paris, a possible reshuffle of all his ideas.

Stanley was now in the box, efficiently furnishing details of his name, education and career, and almost explaining how it was that he had so mysteriously failed his Smalls. His description of his own indispensability to the ballet nearly brought Stroganoff back hot foot to deny it, while his version of the assistance he had given the police tempted Quill to do the same. Why, said Stanley, it was he who by sheer deduction had found the revolver with which Palook had been shot.

This was the first the court had heard of any revolver and the coroner turned a reproachful eye on Quill. Quill quickly passed up a note stating that the police were not yet ready for this aspect of the case to come out. But Mr. Zzugg was not to be browbeaten. He dismissed Stanley and recalled Quill.

"Did you," he asked, "have the revolver given to you as stated by the last witness?"

"Yes."

"Has it been established as the revolver that killed the deceased?"

"Yes."

The coroner paused before putting the vital question. He was aware that Quill did not want it asked, but he was not going to let the police bully him into suppressing all the more interesting evidence.

"Has the owner of the gun been traced?"

Quill was furious. "Yes."

"What is his name?"

"The police would prefer not to disclose it at the moment."

"Is that so? Curiously enough," said the coroner mildly, "I was under the impression that I was conducting this inquest—not the police."

He was asking for it, thought Quill. All right, he would get it.

"His name was Pavel Bunia."

The effect was extraordinary. For the first time in the history of the Ballet Stroganoff, you could have heard a pin drop.

"The man who was killed last night?" said the coroner hollowly.

"Exactly," said Quill. "Are there any further questions you would like to ask?"

"No—no."

There was another scuffle at the Press table.

Quill stepped down leaving the coroner a prey to conflicting emotions. By his own insistence he had unearthed a sensational piece of evidence, but if he followed it up, it was likely to result in a verdict of murder against a person who had himself been murdered. Could he risk this anomaly? Mr. Zzugg decided he could not.

Proceedings now took on a quieter note. There was nothing in the demeanour of Shura Lubova to suggest the vixen of the dressing-room last night. She gave her evidence with composure and spoke of the dead man without rancour or warmth. She admitted to having been on the balcony on the night of his death—where she had no right to be. One of the company had a migraine and Shura, out of pure kindness of heart, had allowed her to lie down in her dressing-room and had taken her place.

"Eight or nine girls in a dressing-room, it is not good for migraine."

Who was the girl? Her name was Anna Szonnova and she was still unwell. Certainly the coroner and the police could have her address. Doubtless the management would know it.

"Is it not unusual for a star dancer to deputize for a walker-on?"

"I did not think about it. The girl was unwell."

"Were you on the balcony when deceased was shot?"

"I left it with other dancers a few moments previously."

"You did not while on the balcony notice anything that might help the court?"

"Nothing."

"You did not like the dead man?" said the wily Mr. Zzugg.

"Nobody liked him," Shura answered. There was still no rancour in her voice.

The coroner dismissed her and called the next witness. This was Puthyk. Quill, himself, was vaguely uncertain why he had caused the old man to be subpœnaed but Puthyk took his importance for granted. He beamed affably at the coroner, the jury and the Press. He beamed at Arenskaya and Quill. He beamed at Stroganoff. He even beamed a trifle absently at Nevajno.

"Your name," said the coroner, "is P. Puthyk?"

"*Oui.*"

"You are a dancer in the Ballet Stroganoff?"

"Assuredly. My legs they get a little tired but my elevation it is perfect."

"Quite."

Puthyk turned triumphantly in the direction of Stroganoff. "You see. That one he understands."

"You are a small part dancer?" said the coroner tactlessly.

"Who say that?" Puthyk swung round again while Stroganoff tiptoed guiltily towards the doorway.

"It is true," Puthyk explained to the court, "that now I dance only small parts, but it was not always so. At the Maryinsky . . ." and before the coroner could stop him he had plunged into a recital of his triumphs.

". . . and to-night I dance *Coppélia*," he finished. "And after that," he looked hopefully to where Stroganoff had crept in again, "it is agreed that I dance *Petroushka*."

"*Oui, oui,*" said Stroganoff, winking heavily at the coroner.

"*Bon,*" said Puthyk, all affability again. "You shall see then that I am superb. You come too?" he invited the coroner. "You nice man. I give you box."

The coroner intimated that he would like to ask Puthyk a few questions. Puthyk graciously permitted it. His answers were a little vague. He may have been on the balcony that night, but next week he was dancing the main role. Had they not heard? He was anxious to help the court but his role it must come first. He and Woizikovsky. . . .

It was a very tired and disgruntled coroner who eventually addressed the jury. The inquest had not proceeded on the lines he had visualized. Instead of holding the centre of the stage as he had intended, he had been thrust firmly off it by the powerful personalities of the various witnesses. Instead of handling the witnesses, the witnesses had, for the most part, handled him. And as for investigating the cause of death, the only time he had come across anything promising he was brought to a full stop by the murder of the suspected person. In fact, he was robbed of everything save the prosaic direction to the jury to bring in a verdict of wilful murder against person or persons unknown. This he did, skating carefully over the thin ice of the discovery of the revolver.

The jury duly obliged.

CHAPTER XIII

THAT evening Quill sat in his rooms covering page after page of foolscap with schoolboy handwriting.

"When in doubt," counsels the Detective's Handbook, "document your facts and stare them in the face." Quill had followed this counsel. After some work he found himself looking at the following: *Petroushka*. Three dancers who danced, or were due to dance, this role have died within the past two months.

Feb. 2. Marius Pilaff found shot in dressing-room of theatre in Paris. Verdict—suicide.

April 6. Anton Palook shot on top of booth in last scene of *Petroushka* at the Collodium theatre. Verdict—murder by person or persons unknown.

April 8. Pavel Bunia found shot in booth in first scene of *Petroushka*. Inquest not yet fixed.

The following facts have been established concerning each of the deaths:

Death of Pilaff.

Pilaff was found dead in his dressing-room just before a performance of *Petroushka*, the ballet in which he was dancing the main role, was due to start. Revolver in hand. Verdict of suicide but no good reason for suicide ever discovered. Further particulars may be to hand from Paris Police shortly.

Death of Anton Palook.

The shot was not fired at close quarters and it has not been found possible to fix the exact range or direction. Might have been fired from any part of the house—except gallery and upper circle. Most probable positions for firing unobserved, however, are (*a*) the balconies flanking the sides of the stage, (*b*) the stage boxes.

A revolver, subsequently proved to be the weapon that killed Palook, produced by Stanley Simpson, who claims to have found it in waste-paper basket in Pavel Bunia's old dressing-room. Revolver identified by gunsmith as one purchased by Pavel in his shop on August 17, 1935.

The following are known to have motives of sorts for the murder:

Rubinska. In love with Palook but discarded. Had made an attempt at reconciliation while in the booth during the performance, which had been roughly repulsed. State of mind probably suitable for murder. Evidence, however, shows that she was in her dressing-room at the time of the shot. (Confirmed by her mother, Kasha Ranevsky, and Arenskaya.)

Shura Lubova. In love with Pavel Bunia who had come under the influence of Palook. Had deputized for one of the company on balcony, but claims to have left latter before the shot. No witnesses positive enough to confirm this.

P. Puthyk. Wife unfaithful with Palook. Ancient history now. Further Puthyk, when matter was mentioned, exhibited none of the reactions of a jealous husband nurturing a grudge. On balcony during the performance. Time of descent unestablishable. Puthyk vague and nobody noticed his coming down.

Stroganoff. Fear that Palook would leave him for Lord Buttonhooke. Doubtful if such fear would prompt him to murder, while his accounts of movements, fully checked, left little time over for unobserved shooting practice.

Volti-Subito. Known to dislike Palook. May have more definite grievance. Opportunity to fire unobserved from orchestra pit just possible. First-class shot. (Evidence of Stanley Simpson.)

Stanley Simpson. In love with Rubinska. In wings at time of shooting. Chance of shooting unobserved·extremely remote.

Pavel Bunia. A very strong case of circumstantial evidence surrounds this suspect. Was furiously jealous of Palook's

association with Rubinska. Had quarrelled over it with
Palook in interval. Had gone up on balcony after leaving
stage to stop Appelsinne, who admits he was there with
intent to murder, from shooting Palook. Had taken Appelsinne's revolver, sent Appelsinne away, and stayed behind
himself. Seen by Stroganoff. Means, motive, opportunity—
all complete.

Appelsinne had produced a revolver, unfired and not fitted
with a silencer, which he says is the gun Pavel took from him.
Questioned as to possession of second revolver Appelsinne
stated that Pavel had bought one two years back but that
this had been lost some time ago. This is in all probability
a lie. On the other hand there is only Stanley's word for
it that he found revolver in waste-paper basket.

Evidence considered strong enough to secure warrant for
Pavel's arrest. Arrest postponed at Stroganoff's request till
after performance of *Petroushka*. During performance Pavel
found shot in booth.

Death of Pavel Bunia.

Pavel found shot in booth at 10.45. Seen entering booth
at 10.30 approximately.

Volti-Subito last person to speak to deceased. Observed
talking to Pavel in his booth just before rise of curtain on
Petroushka. Time approximately 10.33. Subito admits coming
on stage for express purpose of making a gibe at Pavel, but
says that Pavel did not answer his remark. It must, therefore,
not be taken for granted that Pavel was still alive when
Subito spoke to him.

It was undeniably possible for Subito to have shot Pavel
while talking to him. There is, however, no shred of evidence
to confirm this suggestion.

Numerous persons passed behind booth during performance,
but it has been found impossible to find any of the company
who will admit to having done so, or to have seen other

people passing. This, however, is clearly accounted for by (*a*) fear of suspicion, (*b*) screening of comrades, (*c*) general lack of observation always prevalent during a stage performance.

Revolver with one chamber fired and fitted with silencer found behind booth. Revolver identified by Stanley as his property which he claims to have missed for the first time that afternoon.

The following have motives—of a kind—for the murder of Pavel:

Shura Lubova. In love with and spurned by Pavel. Uttered threats in dressing-room prior to performance.

Volti-Subito. General dislike—or more as in case of Palook. Had opportunity for the murder—see above.

Kasha Ranevsky. Only man in company with whom Palook was on friendly terms. Nothing to show, however, that Kasha felt particularly friendly to Palook, especially as Kasha is in love with Rubinska, notoriously deflowered by Palook. Claims to have been in dressing-room from rise of curtain till discovery of body, but no external evidence to confirm this. A very far-fetched theory, suggested by the jealous Stanley Simpson, is that Kasha suspected Pavel murdered Palook, and murdered Pavel in revenge.

Stanley Simpson. Sympathy for Shura and public school principles would make Pavel obvious villain in Stanley's eyes. His revolver fired the shot. Did Stanley kill Pavel in mistaken sense of chivalry to save Shura from herself? Then did he also kill Palook to protect Rubinska, with whom he is in love, and then claim to have found revolver in waste-paper basket? Extremely improbable.

But then everything about these murders is improbable.

Theories concerning the murders.

There are two distinct theories.

The first assumes that the two murders and the suicide,

which may have been murder, are inter-related. This assumption is made on the fact that the three dead men were dancing or about to dance the title role in the ballet *Petroushka*.

The second theory is to treat the two murders as independent entities, admitting only that the first may have influenced, or prompted, the second. Into this theory the Paris suicide does not enter and is, in fact, entirely irrelevant.

The second is the more probable of these theories if only because it permits Pavel to remain suspect for the murder of Palook. The first theory automatically acquits Pavel by reason of his death and reduces the circumstantial evidence against him to mere coincidence. But it is an astonishing coincidence that Pavel should find himself in a position with the opportunity, the means, and possibly the desire to kill, while the real murderer was crouching elsewhere.

Assuming that Pavel killed Palook, Pavel's death might now be the revenge of a friend. Snag is that Palook cannot be found to have had any friends with possible exception of Kasha. A more probable theory is that Pavel was killed by an enemy (he had plenty of these), who had got the idea from the murder of Palook.

Theory that the three deaths are related.

Three dancers in the role of Petroushka have died. Pilaff (dressing-room, Paris); Palook (shot at end of third scene in *Petroushka*); Pavel Bunia (shot in booth at beginning of first scene). If there is no connection between the cases it is certainly curious that death should have overtaken the three, while dancing or about to dance *Petroushka*. If there is a connection it argues the presence of a person in the company with an antipathy for all *Petroushkas*. For this antipathy to extend to homicide argues a madman.

Detective's Handbook not helpful in this respect. "Watch carefully for indications of an unbalanced mind." But the entire Stroganoff company showed strong indications of unbalanced minds a dozen times daily.

Reticence is not one of the qualities of Russian dancers, but so far have not encountered any persons revealing a dislike of *Petroushka* in their speech. It seems to be a favourite part and much coveted by dancers. Even old Puthyk, in spite of his age, still hankers after it.

Assuming there is a *Petroushka* hater in the company, would he or she not give themselves away every time they spoke of the ballet. There can be no harm in discussing the ballet with various members of the company and noting the reactions.

* * * * *

As he looked at the last entry it struck Quill that it was a pity that the murders had not taken place during a ballet by Nevajno. By all accounts the place was bristling with people who did not like Nevajno's ballets. Quill smiled at the idea. From there his thoughts passed to Nevajno himself.

Immediately Quill felt slightly excited. Not that Nevajno was any madder than the rest, but his mania lay in a passion for the modern, combined with an extreme sensitiveness of any disparagement of his own work. A ballet like *Petroushka*, though created as late as 1910, might easily appear to Nevajno as old and absurd—and its obstinate success might easily breed a hatred of it, which in turn might translate itself into a hatred of the performers in it.

On the more prosaic question of opportunity, Nevajno had not been dancing in the ballet when Palook was killed. As there was then no possible reason to rank him among the suspects, his statement that he had been in the wings had not been closely checked. When Pavel was murdered Nevajno was dancing the Moor and occupied the next booth but one to Pavel. This offered an opportunity of slipping out for a moment, shooting Pavel, and slipping back again.

If this was the crime of a lunatic there could be no better suspect. However, psycho-analysis was not one of his strongest points and it might be as well to have an expert opinion when tackling Nevajno.

Reasonably satisfied with the night's work, Quill put away his notes and went to bed.

CHAPTER XIV

SCOTLAND YARD was not the only body to get in touch with Paris over the matter of Marius Pilaff's suicide; the whole of Fleet Street had had the same idea. But while the connection between the three dead Petroushkas was only one of alternative theories to Quill; to the Press, unhandicapped by the need of making an arrest, it had become a burning faith. In some mysterious way the dead clowns seemed to have altered the face of London. Every small tobacconist-and-sweet shop had its bulgy window propped up with some such inviting tit-bit as "Death Stalks the Ballet." "Three Clowns No Longer Laugh." In trains, bobbing eyes focused on "The Ballet with the Trail of Blood." At home, dressing-gowned wives shuddered delightfully over composite pictures of the three Petroushkas hunched upon the stage, and strongly suspected Stroganoff of being the bluebeard, mainly on account of his foreign name. Newsboys, the latest details strapped to their persons, ambled blissfully through the streets, and the head waiter at the Hotel des Gourmets so far forgot himself as to swop a theory with a customer who had asked for sausage and mash.

The *Night Despatch* hurriedly abandoned its series of "Latter-Day Landrus" in favour of "Tragedies in Sawdust" (Petroushka, Pierrot, Pagliacci, etc.).

"Three Crumpled Clowns," flaunted the *Daily Distraught* posters.

"The Clown With The Cloud of Death," achieved the *Evening Scoop*.

"They Danced Petroushka and Died," announced the *Evening Yelp* pathetically.

"Is There a Hoodoo on This Ballet?" asked the *Mystical Times*.

"Abandon This Ballet," demanded *Fascism for All*.

"Ballets, Bullets, Blood . . ." promised a popular weekly.

And then there were long articles, hurriedly commissioned from prominent writers of detective fiction, not one of which omitted to point out that truth was stranger than fiction.

The *Daily Distraught* ran a special by their ace sob-sister, Petunia Patch.

"The terrible fate of the three crumpled clowns cries to the world for vindication. . . . What is this role that brings with it a heritage of doom?

The trail of death is set in Paris—City of Laughter—City of Love! There, huddled in his dressing-gown, his sightless eyes raised to the powerless ceiling, his pitiful hands forever still, crouched the first fated clown, Marius Pilaff (who was, of course, first cousin to the well-known diplomat, Prince Andrey Andreyev). Known to balletomanes the wide world over, for the brilliance of his *tours en l'air en seconde*.

In London, Anton Palook (whose Petroushka ranked second only to that of Nijinsky, Bolm, Woizikovsky, Massine, Lichine, Shabelevsky and Wilzak) met his death in full view of a brilliant first-night audience.

Petroushka, the comic figure of a thousand Russian fairings, Petroushka, the tragic hero of a ballet weighted with tears. Petroushka—No man and Everyman. Petroushka, high on the roof of the blue-fringed booth, his mimed agony turning suddenly to the pangs of a terrible death . . . the second clown is a crumpled shape against the deep shadows of a painted world.

And still the grisly tally has not been concluded. . . .

Behind the curtains of the puppet's booth—hiding what dreadful secret? Screening what cunning hand? The finest dancer of them all[1] lurches against the canvas walls. His features are still, beneath the running grease paint. His mouth has sagged horribly. Pavel Bunia has met a death more secret, perhaps more terrible, than any of those fated clowns.

Public opinion may question the propriety of giving *Petroushka* at the Gala Stroganoff, which has been promised for April 14th, but the determination of the management remains unshaken. All London will be gathered to do honour to the Grand Old Man of Russian Ballet—Benois himself.[2] 'It is inconceivable,' said the manager of the theatre, Mr. Montague Saintly, 'that *Petroushka*, his greatest work, should not be given.'

The ballet of the world would be the poorer for the banning of *Petroushka*, and the ballet of the world, it must go on![3] But who will be willing to dance Petroushka—who will flout the chain of death?

Perhaps it will be only in the hearts of those who have known and loved the ballet that Petroushka's voice will be heard screaming its dumb indictment to the silent sky. For all Russians are grown-up children—laughter-loving children —with a child's love of make-believe and a child's fear of darker things. And what could be darker, more eerie, and more pitiful than the memory of those three dead clowns, strung on that mysterious, that tragic chain?

'Who is to be the next Petroushka?' the dancers ask each other, 'and what will happen to him?'

In what familiar guise does death stalk the Ballet, these children of superstition cry? And who will be foolhardy enough to take the role on Wednesday week?

[1] Poet's licence.
[2] "If 'e come"—Stroganoff.
[3] Pardonable lapse due to constant button-holing of Stroganoff.

Who brave enough?

Who?"

Stroganoff was sick of the question. The waiter who brought his chocolate in the morning. The commissionaire who called his taxi. The stage-doorkeeper at his theatre. Sundry members of his company lingering about the stairs. Mr. Saintly with his enquiring pince-nez bobbing outside his office door. Hiram B. Sausage with Fleet Street at the other end of the line. And finally, the unescapable Stanley, arriving early and clamouring for his answer.

To make it worse he had not the faintest idea who *was* going to dance Petroushka.

*   *   *   *   *

Ernest Smithsky was his most experienced dancer now, but it was impossible to visualize Smithsky as Petroushka. Or rather only too easy to visualize that grim conscientiousness, pirouetting as faultlessly and as unemotionally as a whirling top. Still, Smithsky was a coward, he would probably be only too relieved not to be offered the part. But his other dancers were almost as unsuitable. The only one of his younger members who showed any signs of talent was Kasha Ranevsky.

Stroganoff remembered suddenly that he had promised the part to P. Puthyk to keep him quiet at the inquest. Puthyk must be told at once not to take the promise too seriously— at any moment he might go and make the announcement to some reporter. It would not be pleasant breaking the news to the old man. Bright idea—he would tell Stanley to do it!

"But you be tactful—no?" he finished.

What was that clever English axiom about breaking off two glass houses with one stone, reflected Stroganoff happily as Stanley departed. Certainly he had achieved it this time. Life perhaps was not so complicated after all. His ballet was a sensation as never before; all seats sold weeks ahead and the management actually asking him to extend his season. For the first time for many years he saw himself solvent. What with his profits and those gold shares he had bought last week that would soon be double, he would be rich and prosperous; and his broker, he would at last be polite. "I ring him up now," he promised himself, "and find out how they are feeling."

But here was M'sieur Quill, doubtless in a very good humour over the new assassin that he must find. Stroganoff pushed away the receiver and produced his usual welcome.

Quill replied shortly that he had not slept at all.

"Me, when I cannot sleep," said Stroganoff irrepressibly, "I hum to myself 'Otchi Tchernia.' It go like this. . . ."

Quill stopped him. "Not now. I've come to ask you some questions."

Stroganoff was instantly depressed.

"Useless to come to me and ask who dance Petroushka next. It is a problem *bien difficile*. First we have none who can dance it good, and second, if we should find such a one he would be afraid. All my dancers think that when they dance Petroushka next they die. It is your newspapers that have done this thing to me." Indignantly he picked up the *Daily Distraught*, brandished it and threw it into the waste-paper basket, only to rescue it the next moment. "My shares, they are in that!"

"I would like a few details about Pilaff's suicide," said Quill, and Stroganoff sighed.

"If he were only alive my problem it would not exist. He was superb as Petroushka. Not as superb as Woizikovsky, but better much than Anton Palook."

The 'phone bell rang.

"*J'écoute*," said Stroganoff. "I am dancing him myself," he finished fiercely.

"I would like to hear your own account of Pilaff's death."

Stroganoff shrugged. "It was strange. Pilaff very nice man. He laugh, he joke, the girls they all like him and never he ask me for the advance. And then . . . poof! he suicided. It is the mystery insoluble."

"Did he, to your knowledge, have any enemies?"

"*Mais non!* We all love him—except maybe Nevajno. Nevajno a little cross because Pilaff he never consent to dance in his ballets. Pilaff old-fashioned and would never dance anything later than Fokine."

"And that upset Nevajno?"

"What would you? Nevajno is an artist. He lives only for his work. To ignore it, to dismiss it as Pilaff did—that is the insult. Nevajno so hurt with Pilaff he never even ask him to schange him scheque."

After Quill's speculations about the modernist, this was distinctly interesting.

"Was Nevajno in the theatre on the night of the suicide?"

"*Mais pourquoi pas!* All the company it was there. Anton and Pavel they share a dressing-room then," he remembered, "but it was not a success."

"Was the personnel of your company the same in Paris as in London?"

"*Absolument,*" said Stroganoff with pride. "My company they never leave me—I am to them like a father. Sometimes," he admitted reluctantly, "there is a little exception—but then, children they sometimes quarrel and leave their fathers too. But my principals they never go—not even to Button'ooke. Especially," he added naively, "now that I shall be able to pay them. And that remind me." He dialled.

"I desire," he said, " M'sieu Johns. Is this M'sieu Johns? Good mornings. I am Stroganoff. You remember me without doubt. My shares they feel well—no?"

"No!" he repeated, startled. "*Tiens! c'est curieux!* Still, it can't be serious. Doubtless they will get up soon, Maybe it is good idea to buy some more? . . . No! but, *mon ami,* you are too cautious. Do you not realise that to make money you must risk something?"

But the broker appeared to be adamant and after some further protests Stroganoff hung up.

"He advise me to sell," he confided indignantly. "What you think of that? If I sell to-day I lose already fifty pouns."

"You do not consider," said Quill, trying hard to bring him back to the point, "that Pilaff did not commit suicide? That he was murdered?"

Stroganoff did not seem interested. "Per'aps, but that was long time ago and in Paris. So why you worry? Me, I must worry first for a Petroushka for Wednesday week. That it will not be Ernest Smithsky I am determined. I go now to frighten him good." And carefully folding the *Daily Distraught* at Petunia Patch's Crumpled Clown article, he strode off to drop it carelessly in Smithsky's dressing-room.

Quill let him go. There was no help to be got out of Stroganoff this morning. Only one person in the company could be relied upon to remember the details of a three-months'-old death, and that was Stanley. Quill set off to find him.

Stanley, found, had forgotten nothing. There was not a single detail of his sojourn in Paris that he did not remember and attempt to retail, including an irrelevant story of an expensive adventure of incredible purity in the foyer of the Folies Bergeres. As to the death of Pilaff, Stanley's chief emotion seemed to be one of irritation at the Surete, who had not allowed him to help. He himself had never been satisfied with the suicide verdict. Not that he particularly suspected anyone, but he had been given no chance to investigate.

"I tell you what," said Stanley, tapping Quill's chest impressively, "I've come to a conclusion. There is a murderer in this company."

"No!" said Quill.

"There's something fishy about three dead clowns."

Stanley, too, had read Petunia Patch. "Seems to me most likely that one person did in all three. And what's more I have a theory as to who it is. Don't ask me about it," he went on quickly. "I don't want to talk about it till I've got proof—and I hope to have proof soon."

"Oh," said Quill.

"It's dangerous, of course, but I'm used to danger. And directly I've got the evidence I'll let you know."

"But," began Quill.

"Don't thank me," said Stanley, "I'm only doing my duty as a citizen."

Quill left him to his researches, in which curiously enough he felt no great confidence, and went out to lunch.

*   *   *   *   *

Quill returned to the Collodium that afternoon to find the foyer besieged by Balletomanes—rather small Balletomanes with rather smart Mammas. Saturday afternoons were scholars' afternoons at the Ballets Stroganoff.

On the whole the gathering was more sedate than those that were wont to muster on grown-up occasions.

True, the corridors were awhirl with socked and coated ballerinas rotating imitatively, but the Collodium is by no means unique in harbouring this touching sight. How often has the foyer at Covent Garden itself offered the pleasing spectacle of a boiled-shirted balletomane, pink but persevering, poised winsomely on one toe while the other descries all manner of involved sequences? True, the younger set came armed with a battery of cushions, but again the Collodium Juvenilia is by no means unique in this respect, for how many baffled balletomanes have, in their day, perched upon the pursed-up ledge of their seat at Covent Garden—a ledge that wheezes and whangs and collapses at the most embarrassing junctures.

Quill, making his way through the bobbing sea of curls,

spotted Stroganoff beamingly at anchor by the box office. Evidently the balletomane of the future was more to his taste than the balletomane of the past. Besides, he had just succeeded in shunting a local Mamma, who would be forced now to show her sheaf of pictures to the pinned-down Stanley. In a burst of well-being Stroganoff turned to the nearest unknown in the bobbing sea and patted its disgusted head.

"So you came to see the *Casse-Noisette* Stroganoff?"

"Worse luck!" The unknown hunched his shoulders.

"What!" said the impresario astounded. "You do not like the *Casse-Noisette* Stroganoff?"

"No."

Light began to dawn. "It is perhaps that you prefer the *ballet sérieux? Sylphides—Oiseau de Feu—Petrou*—that is to say, *Lac des Cygnes?*"

"No," said the unknown firmly.

Stroganoff tried again. "You clasp me by the leg. Next you will be telling me that you prefer *le Cinéma!*"

The unknown nodded eagerly.

"*Le* Meeckymouse?" enquired Stroganoff. But this, it appeared was "Cissie." What the unknown yearned for was something modern, something that had a relation to life as it was lived in the Bowery. Tough-guy stuff

"Then," said Stroganoff sagely, "you will like well the choreography Nevajno. *Très* Tough-guy. *Bien* bump-off. I give you ticket if you like for *Gare-du-Nord*. It is a masterpiece you tell me—and I will not contradict."

He produced a white slip, but the unknown waved it scornfully aside. Defeated, Stroganoff wandered away to bestow his affability elsewhere. Quill went off to the auditorium. It was now merely a matter of time before Stroganoff would be saying: "You have seen *Casse-Noisette*—no?" and it would be gratifying to startle him with an affirmative. Besides this, he was beginning to acquire a sneaking liking for ballet.

He made his way to Stroganoff's box[1] which was occupied by the balleto-medico, gazing sulkily at the fat girl on the stage—surely the largest Little Clara on record. He looked at Quill without seeing him and burst into a torrent of denunciation. Quill received the invective with a nod and settled beside him. He would have been glad to escape elsewhere, but he had remembered his speculations about Nevajno and wanted the opinion of the balleto-medico concerning them.

Eventually the curtain came down to much juvenile applause.

"Appalling," said the balleto-medico.

"Cheer up," said Quill, "it might have been by Nevajno."

"In which case I wouldn't be here."

"You don't like Nevajno?"

"He's mad." The balleto-medico dismissed him from the conversation. But Quill brought him back.

"Mad enough to be certified?"

"Absolutely. If only," said the balleto-medico wistfully, "I had a ballet-loving colleague, I'd see to it myself. Anything to stop the fellow."

"But who, then, would dance the Moor on Wednesday week before Benois himself if he come?" quoted Quill glibly.

The Stroganoff touch awoke the balleto-medico to Quill's presence.

"Oh, it's you," he said in some relief. "I thought it was Stanley."

Quill laughed. "He's busy finding the murderer for me."

"Talking of the murderer," said the balleto-medico with interest, "I've come to the conclusion that I rather admire the fellow. He hasn't killed a good dancer yet. The man has taste. I wish he'd exercise it more often."

"He very likely will."

"Hope so," said the balleto-medico blandly. "You know,"

[1] "Come to my box when you will. I charge you nothing."—Stroganoff.

he confided, "I sympathize with him to some extent. I've often felt like murdering Anton Palook myself after one of his triumphal appearances, and as for killing Pavel before he could lay his hands on Petroushka, why, it was nothing but the action of a public benefactor."

"Am I to take it," asked Quill, "that you believe the Petroushkas were killed because they danced badly?"

The balleto-medico sighed. "I wish I could believe it. It's the sort of censorship the Ballet Stroganoff needs."

Quill took the plunge. "It is one of the police theories that these murders might be the work of a madman."

The balleto-medico saw the point. "You mean there is somebody whom the sight of a Petroushka prompts to homicide?"

"Perhaps."

"Might be something in it," said the balleto-medico thoughtfully. "I had a patient once who felt that way about crooners. But then, his wife had eloped with one."

Quill remembered the Puthyks. "A ballet dancer would hardly mind that."

"Agreed," said the balleto-medico. "On the other hand they can work themselves into passions over matters that, to the tennis club mind, are utterly without importance."

"I've noticed that," said Quill.

"Take Nevajno, for instance. You can't insult the fellow in a normal manner. Call him every name under the sun, sleep with his mistress or slap his face, and the chances are that he won't even notice it. But any slight—real or imaginary —on his work brings him foaming to his feet."

"He must be pretty active when you're about." Quill laughed and proceeded to take advantage of the opening. He explained his suspicions, said he was planning to interview Nevajno the next morning and, pointing out that while the police-surgeon knew a lot about insanity, he knew nothing about ballet dancers and might easily be confused by the somewhat similar symptoms, begged the balleto-medico to accompany him. The latter jibbed a bit, protesting that he had an appointment, that he was not speaking to Nevajno and that anyway Nevajno lacked the taste to have done the murders. But Quill insisted. They wrangled through two acts and it was not the final curtain of *Casse-Noisette* that the balleto-medico capitulated.

They fixed a *rendezvous* for the following morning. Then Quill went off to see Stroganoff.

*   *   *   *   *

Stroganoff stood in an impressive posture in front of the fireplace, his right hand sawing short cuts through the air to register determination and defiance. In front of him, sleekly brilliantined and lolling in an arm-chair, sat Volti-Subito, smiling meaningly at a morning coat that had done its best to look as though it had been cut in Savile Row.

"*Inutile* to argue," Stroganoff was saying as Quill entered. "I am resolute. On the morning after Wednesday week you are sack."

The unruffled Volti selected a fresh cigarette. The morning coat only just refrained from rubbing its hands, and took up a sheet of paper. Quill sat down to watch the entertainment.

"According to clause 7 (*c*) of my client's contract," gabbled the morning coat smoothly, "if the employer shall at any time hereafter commit or endeavour to commit a breach of any kind whatsoever of clause 3 (*d*) hereof, and or/if the conductor shall at any time hereafter commit any such breach as aforesaid of any of the provisions of clause 5 (*e*) hereof and/or if either of them, the employer or the conductor, shall commit any such breach as aforesaid of any term or condition herein contained, other than any term or condition contained in either or both of the said clauses 3 (*d*) and 5 (*e*), then and in any such case the employer shall pay to the conductor, or the conductor to the employer as the case may be, as liquidated damages, the sum of five hundred pounds or its equivalent in whatever currency shall be most expedient, together with interest at the rate of £5 per centum per annum from the date of such breach or from the date when such breach is first discovered, whichever is the earlier, until such time as payment has been made."

"Poof!" said Stroganoff.

"An expensive poof," said Volti nastily.

"I care nothing for the expense," said Stroganoff. "Me—I am an artist. Because my orchestra it is perfect I am glad. But I weep because my conductor he is rotten."

"Slander!" said the morning coat.

"Therefore I say I dismiss my conductor. A bad musician it is a pain in the ear."

"On what grounds," asked the morning coat, still smooth, "do you base your assertion of my client's alleged inefficiency?"

"He do not watch the stage."

"Who would," asked Volti, "when the Stroganoff Ballet is dancing on it?"

Stroganoff drew himself up to his full height.

"You insult my ballet. That," he said, a gleam of hope in his eye, "is the libel. I take the action and get much damages. I, too, have an advocate," he added.

The morning coat smiled quietly.

"You laugh," said Stroganoff infuriated. "You think that you have me in hollow stick—no? You think that I, Vladimir Stroganoff, am helpless with your contracts? That I will pay quietly all that you ask?"

"Not quietly," said Volti.

"But soon you will laugh the other side of your cheek. For I am decided. I pay nothing. Not one *centime*. And if you take me to the Court you will be overcome with sorrow at the things about you that I tell the coroner."

"Judge," said the morning coat, shocked.

"Both," said Stroganoff. "I tell everybody That on Tuesday

E

you double the pace of *Sylphides* and my dancers they are compelled to run. That on Wednesday you forget the cuts in *Lac des Cygnes*. That on Thursday you kill Pavel. . . ."

"What!" said Volti, shaken at last out of his perilous calm.

"It is decided that you kill him," said Stroganoff blandly. "My friend here—M'sieu Quill—just tell me that he arrest you soon." He winked heavily. "*N'est-ce pas?*"

The morning coat slid nearer to the agitated Volti and whispered to him not to worry. "Damages for wrongful arrest," it said, "were worth a fortune."

But Quill was making no arrest that afternoon. He said so. Stroganoff seemed disappointed.

"The police they still have an eye on you," he threatened Volti. "And on Thursday mornings you go."

The morning coat seemed about to start reading again, but changed its mind.

"In view of the special circumstances," it said, " and taking into consideration the fact that my client is almost as anxious to leave your employment as you are to dispense with his services, he has intimated to me his willingness to consider an amicable settlement for a sum considerably less than that stipulated in the contract."

"*Pardon,*" said Stroganoff.

"It means we'll take two hundred," said the morning coat suddenly human. "And between you and me and the lamp-post. . . ."

"Lamp-post?"

The morning coat became formal again. "That is our final offer. You would be well advised to accept it. If the matter gets to Court it will cost you considerably more than that in costs alone."

Stroganoff reflected. "You watch the stage on Wednesday week," he said to Volti, "and then maybe I think about it."

The interview seemed to have reached as satisfactory a stage as it ever would. Volti nodded and got up.

"Come, Mr. Shapiro," he said to the morning coat. They left, and Stroganoff, relieved, sank back into his arm-chair. He sprang up again the next moment for Stanley had entered.

"Go away," he said.

But it appeared that this was what Stanley wanted. He had come to ask for the evening off.

"*Impossible,*" said Stroganoff promptly. "Who then will lead the applause in the Upper Circle?"

"Doesn't the Upper Circle applaud for itself," asked Quill. This seemed a new angle on stage life.

"For the Ballets Nevajno—no," said Stroganoff. "And to-night we give *Gare du Nord* and Nevajno he is sensitive to *le silence.*"

"But," said Stanley, "I've promised to help the police and I want time off to follow up a most important clue."

Stroganoff looked at Quill incredulously. "You have asked Stanley to help?"

"He's offered," said Quill tactfully.

Stroganoff shrugged. "*Mais mon ami, c'est votre affaire.* In that case I give Stanley the permit, and Appelsinne he can go up and shout '*bis*' instead."

"Not Appelsinne," said Stanley panic-stricken.

Quill suppressed a smile. So Stanley's suspect was the dour Appelsinne. Stanley had got his cast a bit muddled. Appelsinne might have wanted to kill Palook, but he could never have wanted to kill Pavel.

Stroganoff, too, had divined the situation. "You come here to tell me that you suspect my Appelsinne?"

"I am revealing nothing for the moment," said Stanley, the sphinx.

"But you have revealed, *déja,* and the thing it is *rigolo.* Appelsinne to murder Pavel—poof!"

"Stranger things have been known," said Stanley darkly.

"When?" asked the interested Stroganoff.

Quill came to Stanley's rescue. "Have you any proof?"

"Not yet," said Stanley gratefully. "But I'll get that to-night with any luck. I have a plan."

"All right," said Stroganoff. He had tired of this un-profitable discussion. "And meanwhile, you get out—no?"

Stanley got out, and after a discreet interval, Quill followed.

CHAPTER XV

QUILL sat in his room, reading, with a certain amount of jealousy, about an obnoxiously successful French detective, and avoiding night starvation on the rather un-satisfactory gas-cooker provided by Miss Treackle. It was past midnight and Quill was pleasantly tired. The evening at the theatre had been as uneventful as any evening containing a performance of Nevajno's *Gare du Nord* could be. Quill himself had been completely bewildered by the snarling locomotive that sprawled right across the backcloth, the weirdly dressed and unusually agile porters, the boiling of noises in the orchestra pit, and the station master (the choreographer himself) who spent all his time dancing with the more attractive passengers. The action was explained in the programme, but it did not help Quill much to be told that the station was the Universe, the train Fate, and the passengers the nobler emotions of the human soul, such as hatred, jealousy, vanity and greed.

Nevertheless, a part of the audience had seemed to like the ballet. Many of them were on their feet shouting "brava," "superb" and even "Nevajno." But another faction, led by the balleto-medico, sat back in their seats and talked con-temptuously of design, dynamic rhythm, plastic values, grouping and line. Nevajno had made a speech containing a number of gibes at Petipas, and some dark allusions to a new and even more revolutionary work on which he was at present engaged. Listening to him, Quill had found himself anticipating to-morrow's interview with a certain amount of apprehension.

The French detective in Quill's book was just expatiating on psychology to an audience born to be admiring, when a knock on the door, which somehow managed to combine fury and prudery in equal proportions, brought him to his feet.

Miss Treackle, her flannel dressing-gown—a raw pink—tasselled firmly round her waist, her hair braided for the night, gave tongue.

"A lady to see you." The brevity of the sentence was more than compensated for by her expression.

A horrid vision of Arenskaya, an abandoned Russian gipsy, dropping feverish cigarette ends on Miss Treackle's carpet, floated before Quill's eyes.

"Show her up," he said resigned.

"That I won't do," said Miss Treackle firmly. "Really, Mr. Quill, I'm surprised at you. My house has always been respectable. You will see her downstairs in the drawing-room. The fire has gone out but I can't help that."

A week ago Quill would have descended meekly to shiver in front of Miss Treackle's sister's wedding group, a photograph which, in addition to the rather dazed-looking relatives, also included a picture-hatted Miss Treackle, gazing enviously at the not very prepossessing capture of the bride. But now he had been infected with some of the buoyancy of the Ballet Stroganoff. He was damned if he was going to catch cold to please Miss Treackle's furious sense of propriety.

"You will show her up here," he said firmly.

Miss Treackle tightened the tassel of her dressing-gown. "Never under my roof."

"In that case," said Quill affably, "there will be a spare room under it next week. This room," he elaborated.

"Are you giving me notice to vacate?"

"Yes."

Miss Treackle seemed about to snap an acceptance but stopped short. Never late with the rent. Never quibbles about extras. Never questions the laundry bill. Hardly ever in. And anyone else would certainly insist on having the room re-papered.

"Is the lady a relative?" she asked charitably offering a loophole.

"My grandmother," said Quill.

"That," said Miss Treackle, allowing no trace of incredulity to appear on her features, "is different." She stalked out and returned to usher in Rubinska.

"Thank you, Miss Treackle," said Quill.

"Not at all, Mr. Quill." The door snapped to, but not before a scornful "grandmother" had floated through it.

Rubinska was clearly labouring under some emotion. She crossed impulsively to Quill, snatched at his hands, and gazed at him with large pleading eyes. She was altogether adorable.

"You must promise me something."

"Of course," said Quill. In his relief that she was not Arenskaya, he was willing to promise anything.

"You must arrest Kasha Ranevsky at once."

Quill began to revise his views about promises. "Why?"

"To save his life."

"How?"

"Don't you understand," said Rubinska impatiently. "Nothing short of an arrest will stop him dancing Petroushka and then he'll be killed."

"Has Stroganoff offered him the part?"

"Not yet—but he's going to. I know he's going to—everybody says so."

"But surely," said Quill, "if you feel that way you can persuade him to refuse."

"I've tried," said Rubinska. "I've been trying all evening.

But Kasha's too ambitious. He laughs at the danger. He even says there is no danger. And there is—isn't there?"

"There may be," Quill was forced to admit.

"Then you must arrest him."

Quill led her to a chair and fed her a cigarette.

"Take it calmly," he said. "You must realise for yourself that I can't take Kasha into protective custody on the strength of a superstition."

"Then you must order Stroganoff to give another ballet."

Quill explained patiently that Scotland Yard could hardly order the cancellation of a ballet on the grounds that somebody might be murdered in it. They could not afford to advertise their incapacity in this manner.

"Then you will do nothing?"

Quill said every precaution would be taken. Plain clothes men would surround the stage; he was even toying with the idea of introducing some of his men into the crowd scenes. The killer, even assuming he would be at work again, would undoubtedly be caught afterwards.

"But first," said Rubinska, " he will kill my Kasha."

Quill sighed. "Your Kasha. Alas! poor Stanley."

"Poor Stanley," agreed Rubinska. "Should I marry Kasha, he will be inconsolable for at least a day. Already because he saw me kiss Kasha before the performance to-night he has gone drinking with Appelsinne."

Quill laughed. "It wasn't a broken heart that made him do that."

"No?"

"No. He suspects Appelsinne of having murdered Pavel and I suppose the alcohol is to loosen Appelsinne's tongue. But Appelsinne will drink him under the table."

A quaking hand knocked at the door and an agitated finger drew Quill into the passage.

"There's a young man downstairs," hissed Miss Treackle. "He's followed her. This is terrible. What shall we do?"

"Show him up," said Quill.

"No," said Miss Treackle. "I will not have bloodshed in my house. Confide in me, Mr. Quill. Is he her husband?"

"He's going to be," said Quill comfortingly.

"I knew it," wailed Miss Treacle. "Look-out," she added as the beaming face of Kasha came running upstairs.

"She has not left yet?" Kasha enquired.

"She's gone," lied Miss Treackle, game to the last.

"Gone?"

"She's here," said Quill. "It's quite all right," he explained to Miss Treackle. "We're not going to kill each other. This," he could not help adding, "is my grandfather."

Panic left Miss Treackle. She tightened her tassel and bade them an acid good night.

Kasha followed Quill into the room and embraced Rubinska affectionately.

"So she hasn't persuaded you to arrest me," he grinned.

"Not quite," said Quill. "All the same," he added, "why don't you do what she asks and refuse the role?"

"It hasn't been offered to me yet," said Kasha. "If it is I shall certainly take it. I've always longed to dance Petroushka."

Rubinska moaned. "But you'll be killed."

"Why should I be killed? This girl here," he explained to Quill, "seems to think there's some lunatic at large killing off every Petroushka in sight."

"She might even be right," said Quill gravely.

"Even if she is," said Kasha obstinately, "I'm still taking the role if I get the chance. I'd be a fool to miss the opportunity."

"An opportunity you would never had had but for the murders," Quill pointed out.

Kasha nodded. "From that point of view I'm grateful to the murderer. I'd almost commit murder myself to dance that role."

Rubinska shrugged. "You see, he's hopeless."

"Absolutely hopeless," agreed Kasha. "But don't worry.

If I get the role Mr. Quill here will see to it that I'm not killed."

"I'll do my best," said Quill. "My reputation won't stand a third murder."

"You see," Kasha picked up Rubinska's coat and helped her into it. "So now we'll go home and let my guardian get some sleep. Besides I have a taxi waiting."

"Spendthrift," said Rubinska.

"Not at all," said Kasha. "Stanley is going to pay for it."

"Why Stanley?"

"Because he is in it. Tight as a lord."

Rubinska was not at all pleased. "Why did you bring him?"

"Someone had to look after him and get him home," said Kasha. "Only it was rather late and I came here first."

Quill escorted them into the street. From the cab Stanley peered owlishly at him.

"Awfully sorry," he said thickly. "He wouldn't talk."

CHAPTER XVI

For the London season Nevajno had installed himself in a semi-detached studio in Bloomsbury—an insufficiency of isolation which appeared to cause the neighbours occasion for complaint. Quill and the balleto-medico, reaching the mews at eleven o'clock on Sunday morning, had no difficulty in finding it. A scowling garage proprietor led them to a door through which an alarming fanfaronade of discords was penetrating, and callously left them to their fate.

"Prokofiev," said the balleto-medico.

Quill knocked, but, realising immediately that this was a mere waste of time, entered.

Deep in an arm-chair, screened by a cloud of smoke, Nevajno was listening entranced to his portable gramophone.

He was wearing a high-necked Russian blouse of luxurious plum velvet, flannel bags and camel-hair bedroom slippers. He waved a vague welcome at his visitors.

"Sit down," he said. "Listen."

The balleto-medico made himself comfortable on a wicker basket that had once belonged to Stroganoff. Quill selected the collected works of Proust. They listened while the record screeched itself to a close, and it was not until Nevajno showed every sign of putting on the other side that Quill intervened.

"Er," he began.

"Later," said Nevajno. "First we must listen to this. It is by Polyshumudshedshi."

"Prokofiev," contradicted the balleto-medico in his forth-right English way.

"Prokofiev pale compared to Polyshumudshedshi," said Nevajno. "Listen and you will be convinced." He attacked the handle. "It is to this music," he announced, "that I have the idea magnificent for a ballet."

The balleto-medico moved restlessly.

"It is called," said Nevajno oblivious, *Table d'hote*. He started the record. "The action it take place in a restaurant. The backcloth it is a bill of fare. I compose it later—it is decided only that it will be symbolic. On the left is painted the black jacket of the *maitre d'hotel*, on the right, one asparagus."

"And that," said Quill ingratiatingly, as a succession of crunching sounds ruined the morning sunshine, "is the heavy-footed waiters shuffling."

"On the contrary," said Nevajno. "That, it is the celery."

Quill subsided but the balleto-medico took action. He crossed to the gramophone and stopped it. Nevajno looked at him like a hurt child.

"Why you do that?" he asked.

"I've heard enough," said the balleto-medico, "I'm sick of your Universal eaters."

"But they are symbolic." Absently Nevajno picked up

Quill's cigarette, lit his own, and tossed the detective's carelessly into the waste-paper basket.

"Appetites," he explained, "are universal. Man he is hungry for food. The nations they are hungry for territory."

"Appetites," said balleto-medico, "are not balletic."

Nevajno turned to Quill. "Take no notice of that one. The way I do it, you have not to fret. Everything I do is balletic. I could take the *sujet* of the Royal Academy," he boasted, "and in my hands it would become beautiful. And symbolic. And balletic."

"You have never been to the Royal Academy," accused the balleto-medico.

"*Naturellement*," said Nevajno. "It is not necessary. Diaghilev did not go to Persia to commission *Sheherazade*. Balanchine went not to ancient Greece for his *Apollon-Musaguets*. Massine did not visit Hamley's for *La Boutique Fantasque*. And I myself was led blindfolded through the *Gare du Nord*, lest what I might see should influence my ballet."

"That," said the balleto-medico, "is obvious."

"You liked it," said Nevajno pleased. "It is unshackled— *n'est-ce pas?* Untrammelled. *Libre.* Nothing there of the *petit bourgeois* with his season ticket."

"And nothing there of Ballet, either," said the balleto-medico.

The yell of rage that Nevajno let forth told Quill that it was time for him to intervene. He had come here to discover if the genius was mad—not to goad him into it.

"I enjoyed it very much," he said placatingly.

"You enjoyed it," said Nevajno, livid. "This ballet that should shake you to the very soul, this ballet that is an abyss of all suffering, that is black with the despair of the world and the futility of endeavour—you enjoy it."

"Very much," said Quill.

"No doubt," said Nevajno cuttingly, "you enjoy also *Sylphides* and *Petroushka*."

"They are real ballets," said the balleto-medico gloatingly. "Though not, of course," he added, " as performed by the Stroganoff company."

Another scream of rage came from the doorway. It was Stroganoff, almost dropping the package he was carrying in his fury.

"That," he said, "is the libel. It is also not true."

The balleto-medico was amused. "Privileged occasion," he said.

"It is the last privilege you shall have of me," retorted Stroganoff. "From now on you pay for your seat and I see to it myself that they put you behind pillar."

"I would prefer that he do not come to the theatre at all," said Nevajno. "He is Philistine."

"Without a doubt," agreed Stroganoff. He paused for a moment. "Still," he resumed, "it is not to debate with the quacks that I have come to you this morning."

Nevajno was immediately on the defensive. "If it concerns that scheque you schange for me . . ."

"*Mais non, mon cher*," said Stroganoff. "That is all right."

"Olright?" echoed Nevajno incredulously. "The bank they have pay it?"

"Doubtless they will do so shortly," said Stroganoff consolingly. "And if not—poof—it matters nothing. We are artists—you and me—not doctors."

But Nevajno still looked puzzled.

"Look," said Stroganoff, getting busy with his parcels, "I bring you little present. *Foie-gras*." He deposited a package on the table. "Champagne." He produced two magnums. "And a little caviare to tempt the appetite."

Nevajno circled the display warily. "Why you bring me all this?"

"It is the compliment from one artist to another."

Nevajno brooded. To Quill it seemed that something was preying on his mind.

"You schange me small scheque?" he asked in his grimmest voice.

Stroganoff gulped a little but rallied. "*Assurément*," he said.

Nevajno struck the table with his fist.

"*Assassin!*" he roared.

"*Mais non*," said Stroganoff.

"*Mais si*," bellowed Nevajno. "All is now clear. I understand everything. All this champagne—all this artist to artist—it is to murder me. Do you deny that it is to ask me to dance Petroushka that you have come here?"

Stroganoff sat down on a pile of suitcases. It was clear from his expression that Nevajno had guessed correctly.

"There is no danger," he said coaxingly, "and as Petroushka you will be superb."

"I shall not be superb," said Nevajno. "It is a role I do not covet. The ballet it is old fashioned and the symbolism it is for the children."

Stroganoff still pleaded. "If you dance this for me I produce for you the ballet of a million shirts."

"Not the shirts," said Nevajno petulantly. "That was last week. Now I work on new idea. *Table d'hote*. It is magnificent. I will play the music now."

"Er," said Quill.

"Not again," said the balleto-medico.

"Later," said Stroganoff. "You dance Petroushka, and I produce that too."

"What will it benefit me if I am dead?" asked Nevajno.

Stroganoff switched his attack to a new angle. "To die for your art it is the greatest thing of all."

Nevajno nodded. "There I agree. To die for *Gare du Nord* —that is the death glorious. Willingly would I sacrifice myself. But to die for *Petroushka* that is merely silly. I will not take the risk. The ballet of the future it need me too much."

"You obstinate yourself," said Stroganoff.

Nevajno in a few piercing sentences confirmed this suspicion. Stroganoff gave up the struggle.

"In that case," he said nastily, "I take out the scheque from your salary. Also I take back this caviare to give to Kasha."

"You can take your champagne too," said Nevajno defiantly. "And all your friends with you. I desire to work."

But before Stroganoff could collect his bottles, there was an ecstatic shrill from the door.

"Champagne!!!" Arenskaya hurried in. "What is it that we celebrate?"

Puthyk too had reached the table and was examining the bottles lovingly.

"Moet-Chandon," he announced happily. "It is my favourite. I drink to you, my darling."

"Where are the glasses?" demanded Arenskaya, always practical.

"There aren't any," Quill prophesied.

He was right, but the balleto-medico came forward with a quantity of cups. Puthyk opened a bottle.

"To what," repeated Arenskaya, passing up her cup for a second helping, "to what is it you said we drink?"

"We drink to nozzing," exploded Stroganoff, who had been watching the performance with growing irritation. "We just drink, that is all. And now I have no champagne left to take to Kasha."

"It is his birthday?" asked Arenskaya interested.

"No," said the balleto-medico rushing in. "It is the Stroganoff idea of a Petroushka."

"He will not need coaxing that one," said Stroganoff, looking meaningly at Nevajno. "He put his art before everything."

Puthyk looked depressed. "He is very young to die," he said sadly.

This bland assumption by everybody that the next Petroushka would die as a matter of course, wounded Quill's professional pride.

"The Police have the situation well under control," he said.

"He will die," stated Puthyk unimpressed. "The poor young man."

Arenskaya crossed to Quill. "He must not die," she said earnestly. "He is a dancer of great promise. And when I have taught him that he shall not bend the knee when he do the arabesque, nor pinch the arms for the *tour en l'air*, and some dozen other little trifles, he will be the dancer complete. So you must guard him with your life or else the little Rubinska she will claw your eyes out."

The waste-paper basket burst into flames.

They were all mad, decided Quill drearily. One as mad as the other.

CHAPTER XVII

ON Monday Kasha had caviare for breakfast.

He was not very fond of caviare for breakfast and he did not grudge the three reporters who kept him company their share.

The Ballet Stroganoff was still in the headlines. Kasha's acceptance of the role of Petroushka had kept them there. The Sunday news sheets perforce had had to be content with speculations as to whether the ballet boasted any dancer brave enough to take the risk—the Monday Press had found its hero. Kasha Ranevsky was news.

"New Star to Dance Petroushka," said the early editions.

"Kasha Ranevsky to challenge Death."

"Young Dancer in Fatal Role."

"*Il Dance pour l'Amour*," said Paris.

"Aryan Dancer Defies Jewish Killer," gloated Berlin.

"Ballet Dancer to Brave Bumper-off," announced New York.

By lunch time Kasha was startled to find that he had given a special interview to the *Daily Distraught*.

"My art," he had apparently told Petunia Patch, " is to me everything. The Ballet Stroganoff it is like a father. Vladimir Stroganoff is a wonderful man."

The source of this message was easy for Quill to divine. When he ran into Stroganoff during his barren plodding round the theatre that afternoon, the latter not only admitted it, but went so far as to complain of the cutting. "They do not print my picture," he said peevishly.

Evening found Kasha under contract to write the story of his life, loves and art—with a prudent clause appointing an experienced executor to complete the work in the event of premature death. Kasha's feeble protests that he would have no time even to start it, were overruled. The experienced executor, it appeared, could look after that as well.

On Tuesday morning Rubinska joined Kasha in the headlines. Reporters had discovered the friendship between them, forcibly affianced them, and now from every column came floods of information concerning the happy pair. How they had loved each other at first sight. How Rubinska had begged him to renounce the role. And how he had quoted Lovelace at her.[1]

Quill too, as the detective in charge of the case, came in for a certain amount of belated biography. That unfortunate matter of the wrongful arrest was dragged up again, jeers (thinly disguised as sympathy) were levelled at him for permitting Pavel to be murdered under his nose, and it was hinted that, though Kasha might be showing courage in facing death for his art, it was sheer foolhardiness not to insist on a more experienced detective before doing it. Quill bore it all with commendable fortitude, until the self-complacent Hiram B. Sausage complimented him on the publicity he was getting.

[1] " I could not love thee, dear, so much . . ."

"Cash in on it, my boy," he counselled.

"Your management they give you rise for this, no?" asked the interested Stroganoff.

But Quill had stopped thinking about promotion. The continued terror campaign in the Press was fast reducing him to its own level of panic. He had not at first seriously believed in the possibility of a third murder, but now, though his common sense still rebelled, he could think of nothing else. If Kasha were killed his career was finished. But even that worried him less than the responsibility of one human being for another. He was dreading to-morrow's gala. The Snarl was dreading it too. All Scotland Yard was jumpy.

It was ridiculous, this helplessness to prevent a murder before an audience of a couple of thousand people. But it happened twice. And there was nothing to do to prevent it happening a third time, except to have as many men in the theatre as possible and to watch . . . and to wait . . .

The Late Night Finals, hard-up for a fresh angle, starred Madame Rubinska as " Anxious Mother."

"If Kasha is killed," she said, "the effect on my daughter's dancing will be deplorable. My daughter is the greatest dancer since Pavlova. I love Kasha like my own son," she added as an afterthought.

Efforts were made to induce Mr. Rubinska to make a statement. The only fact that emerged, however, was that he was né Rabinovitch. Tactfully the Press refrained from printing this.

Wednesday might have been the morning of an execution, except that Kasha was not permitted to choose his own breakfast. This had to be fixed in time for the country editions. Every step he took during that day was fully reported.

On the whole Kasha stood up manfully to his ordeal. He dealt smilingly with the reporters. He shoved his enormously increased mail on to Stanley. He made friends with the plain clothes men who surrounded his rehearsals. But even he blenched slightly at the nudgings and whisperings that arose from the queue that had waited all night, as he entered the stage door on the afternoon of the final rehearsal for the gala performance that night.

*　　*　　*　　*　　*

In the theatre all was frenzy. The foam of whiskered Generals had been pushed firmly into the dress circle and their places in the wings usurped by cameramen and a director, recently fired from Elstree and snapped up by the Next-Minute News Reel Company. He was there to get a picture of Kasha at rehearsal—ready for his News Reel Obituary. On-the-dot Evans prided himself on his far-sightedness. Provided the murderer did not let him down, this picture would be the scoop of the year. Ecstatically be heard the commentary: "The Next-Minute News Reel Company posthumously presents to you the Dance of Death. This is positively the only action picture of that gallant young dancer, Kasha Ranevsky, whose tragic death we all . . ."

Crash! One of the balconies had collapsed. It had never been designed for ten stalwart policemen and as many of the cast as could crowd themselves into this exciting vicinity.

Sergeant Banner disentangled himself from the wreckage, adjusted a Russian beard, and ambled embarrassed over to Quill.

"How do I look?" he demanded with diffident pride.

"Awful," said Quill candidly and wandered off to be collared by Arenskaya.

"It is 'opeless," she shrilled. "You take them away immediately. Your policemen they ruin my ballet—they will not mingle."

Quill protested. "But they only have to walk about."

"*Mais, mon Dieu,*" said Arenskaya, "'ow they walk! 'Ave you see them?"

"Well—of course, they're not trained dancers."

"That I realise," said Arenskaya. "The audience they will

realise it too. They march like soldiers. It is a sight to break the heart. Better far that Kasha should die than that Benois should see such atrocity."

The balcony had been bolstered up again and such of the company as could be cajoled were clambering on to it. Many refused, doubtless feeling that on such an occasion the privilege of nerves need not be confined to the principals and mothers alone. Storms were brewing everywhere. Always temperamental, the Stroganoff Company had reached the pitch of nervous frenzy. The plain clothes men stood dazed, helpless breakwaters in a sea of emotion. Only Kasha was calm—"the fatalistic calm of the Slav," as Petunia Patch was at the moment 'phoning her office.

Engulfed in his magician's robe, Puthyk sat in the wings, practising his flute. He need only pretend to play it at the performance but he was by nature thorough.

"They have permitted me to dance the Magician," he told Quill with pride. "It is a small role but important. And after Kasha die, doubtless I dance Petroushka."

Volti swung his baton. The breakwaters came to life, marched on to the stage, took up their positions, and almost saluted. The rest of the cast went on jabbering.

In the stalls a cub reporter laughed. They had carelessly forgotten to tell him that this was Art. Now half a dozen mothers did so simultaneously.

Down the centre aisle stalked tragedy. Bald-headed tragedy, face masked in gloom, every gesture a fresh despair. Alarmed, Quill hastened to its side.

"What's up?"

"Ssh!" said Stroganoff and led him out of earshot of the reporters.

"I am desolate," he confided. "Benois he does not come."

"Hard luck," said Quill. "Still, the house will be packed."

"You misunderstand me," said Stroganoff. "It is not for finance that I weep. The finance it is beautiful. It is the blow at my prestige that burn me up. Where there is a gala there must be *un invité d'honneur*. It is too late now to get Chaliapine. It will have to be Lord Button'ooke and he is no artist. Always he ring the telephone."

"Still," said Quill, "the audience comes to see the ballets and not Buttonhooke." Privately he was of the opinion that they were queueing up to see a murder, but this did not seem to be the moment for saying it.

Fresh despair seized Stroganoff.

"And what has the Ballet Stroganoff to show them? Policemen!"

"They are very good policemen," said Quill, a little hurt.

"Do not console me, *mon ami*," said Stroganoff. "I am resigned." He looked at the stage where an intellectual Moor (Nevajno) was condescending to chase Petroushka and brightened slightly.

"Kasha he dance well—no?"

"He is superb." Arenskaya joined the party. "He will be the best Petroushka the Ballet Stroganoff has seen."

Stroganoff was impressed. It was seldom that Arenskaya praised. "That is your opinion?"

"Have I not said so?"

The prospect of at last possessing a first-class dancer banished everything else from Stroganoff's mind. Immediately he became immersed in ambitious plans for the future, which included triumphant seasons at the Paris Opera—The Scala, Milan—and the New York Metropolitan—with a series of specially commissioned ballets by Fokine, Balanchine, La Ninjinska, Massine (triumphantly snatched from a broken-hearted de Basil) and, of course, Nevajno.

"There are not enough police on the stage," he finished abruptly. "My Kasha he must be well protected. Bring plenty more."

"*Mais non!*" countermanded Arenskaya. "You will remove half of these. I, myself, shall go on the stage to watch over

Kasha. I think," she said ruminatively, "I dance the Gipsy."

"*Oie!*" said Stroganoff. "It will tire you," he corrected himself hastily, "and I cannot have my beautiful tire herself."

Arenskaya's face set in familiar lines. "I insist."

Quill fled.

Outside the theatre a newsboy waved a paper at him. Petunia Patch was at it again :

POLICE FOR PETROUSHKA
Detectives Guard Ballet's Tragic Triangle

This afternoon, the last rehearsal of *Petroushka*, the Death Ballet, was held behind locked doors at the Collodium theatre. Only Stroganoff and a few close friends assisted at a *répétition* that must surely be unique in the annals of the Dance, performed by a company stricken with terror.

The Ballet's tragic triangle were mute—the little Rubinska (the Doll) her small pale face and great tragic eyes pleading with death. The Moor, that intelligent young choreographer, Nevajno, almost unnaturally composed, and Kasha Ranevsky, the apex of attention—Petroushka, Calamity's Clown— calm with the fortitude of the true artist, looking death unflinchingly in the face, and daring it to strike.

The calmest figure of all was that of Vladimir Stroganoff. He moved reassuringly among his company—his great family of Russian children—taking with him a message of quiet encouragement.

"Kasha," he told me, "has always been to me a son. If he die, I am desolated!"

Detective Inspector Quill was well in evidence. The tall Adonis of Scotland Yard had turned up to station a detachment of eager young constables, recalled from our Pedestrian Crossings, to guard over Kasha on the famous set.

Arenskaya, *maitresse-de-ballet*, and mother-confessor to the Stroganoff company, turned to me with tears in her eyes. "Kasha is to me as a son—a god-son."

In the stalls I was fortunate enough to snatch a word with Rubinska's mother. This is her message to you :

"Kasha will pull through, never fear. This is his big chance and he means to seize it with both hands. Besides, my daughter will be dancing with him. It is her greatest role. It is not true that la Rubinska is to sacrifice her art to marriage. She will be leaving Stroganoff shortly to form a company of her own, where no doubt Kasha will dance as well. He is a dear boy and looks upon me as a mother."

It is rumoured that a Very Important Person Indeed will be present at the Gala Stroganoff to-night.

Quill thrust the paper into his pocket impatiently. He looked incuriously at the waiting queues. Then he looked again. Somewhere he had seen those faces before—that despondency lit by a hungry gleam. Suddenly he remembered. It was outside the Old Bailey.

They were here to see a murder!

* * * * *

There was an ugly undercurrent in the house that night. It whispered through the stalls, murmured through the dress circle, and broke into open speculation in the gallery. There were many in the audience who had never seen a ballet before, but then neither had they ever seen anybody murdered, and they were cheerfully willing to submit to the first in the hope of the second. Their eagerness contrasted sharply with the anxiety of the regular balletomanes. The latter all had the air of having been drawn to the theatre almost against their will. There was none of the frantic discussion, the keen dissension, and the brittle cooing of friendly enemies, that characterises the more normal evenings of ballet. They looked uneasily at each other or shuddered their mutual disgust as some sensation-lover found temporary diversion in gazing at them.

Even the programme girls were in a state of tension. Nobody bought chocolates.

At eight-twenty, Lord Buttonhooke arrived, alighting from his Rolls Royce, an Ermine on one arm, a Sable on the other, behind him a secretary. He was the sort of man who offers you caviare and is mildly surprised if you eat it all. They swept grandly past the welcoming Stanley and established themselves in the Royal Box. A moment later the secretary was 'phoning the office on the apparatus that had been specially installed that afternoon. He was telling them that nothing had happened yet.

Stroganoff wandered in, made a vague speech of welcome[1] and wandered out again.

"What a sweet old man," said the Ermine.

"Poof!" said the Sable in unconscious plagiarism.

Meanwhile, the Old Bailey portion of the audience had found to their disgust that *Petroushka* was not the only item on the programme. Before the murderer could reasonably be expected to get busy, they would have to sit through two ballets. Mournfully they studied their programmes.

"*Les Sylphides*. A choreographic poem in the form of a Reverie."

What was all this?

The lights were lowered. Volti rapped sharply with his baton on the conductor's desk. The curtain was a dark stain screening the stage. The reassuring notes of Chopin floated out to the house. The ballet-goers relaxed. Nothing could be really wrong with a world where they still danced *Sylphides*.

"Pretty," said an Old Baileyite approvingly as the curtain went up.

But half-way through he got restless.

It was not a good performance of *Sylphides*. The movements were jerked, the soft lines turned to angles. It was danced

[1] "It is a great honour that you come, but Benois he would have been better."

by a cast that was afraid. The moonlit glade was oppressed with a general anxiety.

Nobody was really sorry when the curtain swished down to the usual polite applause.

Buttonhooke's secretary was on the 'phone. The news editor was sharp. Would they kindly refrain from disturbing him until something had happened. The alternative story was already set up, anyway.

To Quill, the interval seemed endless. He wandered unhappily back-stage, smiled wanly at Nevajno's frantic directions to the scene-shifters, evaded Arenskaya with a practised neatness, exchanged a few reassuring words with his men, and wandered back into the auditorium.

"*Ajax*. An allegoric fantasy in one act. Choreography by Nevajno."

The Old Baileyites suffered patiently as Ajax leapt his defiance over the miscellaneous collection of rocks. There seemed a sporting chance that he might stumble over one of then and break his neck.

In his dressing-room Kasha sat talking to Rubinska. The sympathetic Sergeant Banner, on guard, pretended not to listen.

Kasha was making an effort to appear light-hearted. Rubinska had given up pleading. She, too, was calling on her courage.

They were arguing about their wedding. Kasha was stating firmly that nothing would induce him to invite Petunia Patch. Rubinska said nothing would persuade her mother not to.

Stroganoff's shining dome bobbed round the door.

"You are ready—no?"

Together Stroganoff and his two children wandered arm in arm down the corridor.

CHAPTER XVIII

FOR once Volti-Subito was watching the stage. The music fell keenly on the ear. The noises of the fair bore an added message of excitement to-night. The shifting and drifting of the crowd began. As they passed they eyed each other warily. So many extras on the stage to-night. So many possible killers.

The street dancers went through their routine. They were keyed up. The crowd caught something of their excitement. Against their will the ballet-goers were infected by their emotion. This was a real performance of *Petroushka* that the Ballet Stroganoff was giving.

The Old Bailey-goers shifted restlessly. "Is that him?" they asked, every time a fresh dancer appeared in the centre of the stage.

Engulfed in his robe, Puthyk bobbed out between the curtains of the Puppet's booth.

"The Magician," explained an assiduous programme reader in the Upper Circle.

The Magician piped his wily tune. The curtains parted. The puppets lolled inanimate in their cells. The Doll, eager in her stillness, the Moor lackadaisical, and Petroushka, his face so quiet it might have been a mask.

"They're all dead!" The all-night wait had proved too much for someone in the gallery.

"Pip-pip." The Moor came jerkily to life.

"Pip-pip." The Doll was on her points.

"Pip-pip." The malevolent magic twitched Petroushka to his feet.

A sigh of relief came from Quill. The Old Baileyites on the other hand felt mildly cheated to find Petroushka still alive.

However, there was plenty of time yet, they reflected. Three more scenes. Three more chances.

"God! He's dancing well," murmured the balleto-medico, peering round his pillar.

Kasha was inspired. He was dancing with the wild abandon of the dupe who is not master of himself, who twitched to order in a dictated frenzy he had no power to subdue. Through him the Doll became something more than the controlled mistress of her feet, and even the Moor lost his detachment and acquired something of the clownish savagery of Fokine's conception.

The applause as the curtain came down was terrific. The house had almost been trapped into forgetting the impending murder.

*   *   *   *   *

" Ah!—*le rideau!*"

*   *   *   *   *

A dominant hand pushed Petroushka into his cell. He was quivering, but still alive.

He hammered the walls of his personal hell, mouthing his misery at the image of the magician above him. His arms move, but they are only sawdust. His legs support him, but they are not real. His feet are but two black rag blobs. His heart loves the Doll, but it does not beat.

Kasha was a poignant as well as a passionate Petroushka. The lines of his agony were painted on his face. The feeling of his agony weighed every gesture. His hysterical welcome of the Doll startled even Lord Buttonhooke into a shudder.

Terrified, the Doll fled from Petroushka's clumsy embrace.

*   *   *   *   *

"*Epatant*," said Arenskaya.
"*Terrifique*," said Stroganoff.

*   *   *   *   *

The scene between the Moor and the Doll was almost a relief. The Old Baileyites laughed at the Moor's antics with his coco-nut. By dint of persuading himself that this was symbolic, Nevajno was putting up quite a creditable performance.

The humours of the *pas-de-deux* went across with a bang. Here were two characters straight out of a comic strip. But into their laughter cut the scream of Petroushka.

"He can conduct that one—when he wants," said Stroganoff approvingly.

In a white rage of jealousy Petroushka leapt at the pair on the sofa. The Moor sprang up. The rivals clinched in a rough and tumble.

The Doll fainted ballet-wise on the sofa—one leg in the air.

*   *   *   *   *

In the wings stood the magician. He was almost in tears.

*   *   *   *   *

Back to the fair. The rhythm in the orchestra heightened, the rhythm on the stage quickened. The music lashed at the excited crowd. A pair of dancing gipsies took the centre of the stage. Neither of them was Arenskaya. (For once she had lost an argument). They danced. A band of nursemaids fluttered their handkerchiefs. The bear lurched ominously across the stage. The coachmen flung themselves wildly into a Russian dance. And everywhere carnival figures jerked their grotesque heads. Snowflakes fell softly on the whirling crowds.

The audience was deadly still.

At the back of each balcony stood a cluster of policemen. Watching.

A tremor passed through the curtains of the puppet booth. Their folds blew open. The orchestra screamed. The puppets leapt on to the stage. Round and round leapt Petroushka. Faster, faster came the Moor, scimitar in hand. Faster, faster, until at last the scimitar cut through the air and Petroushka lay stretched on the ground. Horrified, the crowd edged close. The piping voice of Petroushka mouthed its pathetic farewell.

"Dead?" asked a man in the Upper Circle as the crowd screened the figure from sight.

They sent for the magician. He came to lift a sawdust effigy from the spot where Petroushka had died. Reassured, the crowd drifted off, leaving the old man trailing his rag puppet across the ground.

High on its booth the spirit of Petroushka arose, screaming defiance at the tortured world.

Now! A dozen backs straightened in their seats.

Something was wrong with the magician. His mouth was working. He reeled as though the strength had gone from his legs. Something fell from his hand and clattered on to the stage.

"It is no use," said Puthyk pathetically. "I cannot shoot him. He dance too well."

*   *   *   *   *

Lord Buttonhooke strode from the theatre, a disappointed man.

EPILOGUE

LETTER from Vladimir Stroganoff to Detective-Inspector Adam Quill.

Grand Hotel de la Bazouche,
May. . . .

Mon cher Monsieur Quill,

How are you? This is to tell that the Ballet Stroganoff will soon be in your lovely England once more, doubtless for a season even more triumphant than the last. Alas, that we could not secure Covent Garden. But that is for another year.

With us all is well. Kasha and Rubinska they are long time married—they dance better every day. But me I do not tell them this lest their mother ask for bigger contracts. Volti he is the reformed character—he always watch the stage now. No one is dead since London.

We are bringing with us a big new ballet by Nevajno. It is called *Civilisation*. It is symbolic. There is a scene where the *corps de ballet* is shot with a machine-gun. London will be shaken.

And now, *mon cher*, I want to ask of you one big favour. It concerns my poor Puthyk. I know, *mon cher*, that you do not feel so warm towards the old one as I do. I know that he give you lots of trouble and much anxiety. But remember, M'sieu Quill, he is not *le vrai assassin*—he kill for his art. Petroushka, it was to him his life. He was with Fokine when he invent it. To see it dance bad was more than he could bear. And then he had the delusion. Always he saw himself young, his wife beautiful—it was natural that he should come to think that he alone in the Ballets Stroganoff could bring to the role all that it demanded. We, in the Stroganoff company, knew this well— never were we unkind to the old man when he asked for the part.

(They might have told me, reflected Quill, a trifle bitterly).

157

Often I reproach myself that I did not do as he ask. But no it was impossible. And poor Puthyk he think that I am blind—obdurate. So he decide that all who dance Petroushka shall die until in the end only he is left to take the role. It is a situation *bien ridicule*, but poor Puthyk he reason that to kill for his art it is not crime.

First he kill Pilaff in Paris, but we all think it suicide. Then he stay up on the opposite balcony and shoot Anton. And still we do not suspect him. Even you, Mr. Quill, who are trained to catch assassins, did not suspect. And still the old one he do not get his role. So he say to himself—this Pavel—he is a dancer mediocre, good to support the ballerina, but he has not the fire for Petroushka. It is a crime against art that he dance it. Poof! I kill him before he can begin. And that, M'sieu Quill, is why he shoot Pavel in his booth.

And then he decide to kill my Kasha. Petroushka it is not for the inexperienced. Petroushka he bear the whole philosophy of life. But when the time come Kasha has danced the role well. The old man is a connoisseur. He sees the role is safe in the ballet while Kasha he is with us. For himself he cares no more. And so he does not shoot.

You will understand now *mon cher* Quill, that it is not an assassin, but an artist, that you have put in that pretty home in Sussex. They tell me he is happy. He write often to Arenskaya. All the time the ballet it goes on in his mind, and often he dance Petroushka to the other guests.

You will do me the favour, M'sieu Quill, if you go down to prepare my Puthyk for our coming. He will no doubt give you the welcome royal. Always he speak kindly of you in his letters. Tell him that we will come and see him often and that the Ballet Stroganoff still go on.

> *Mille remerciements,*
> *Gardez-vous bien,*
> V. STROGANOFF.

Rubinska send her love.

With a sigh Quill put away the letter and returned to his notes on the case on which he was engaged. Somehow it was difficult to work up a real enthusiasm over the fate of a vanished laundry van.